S0-BON-852

PONDER

A Romance Novel of the Old West

Phonograph Jones

DISCARD

Volusia County Public Library
1290 Indian Lake Road
Daytona Beach, FL 32124

The contents of this work, including, but not limited to, the accuracy of events, people, and places depicted; opinions expressed; permission to use previously published materials included; and any advice given or actions advocated are solely the responsibility of the author, who assumes all liability for said work and indemnifies the publisher against any claims stemming from publication of the work.

All Rights Reserved
Copyright © 2017 by Phonograph Jones

No part of this book may be reproduced or transmitted, downloaded, distrib-uted, reverse engineered, or stored in or introduced into any information storage and retrieval system, in any form or by any means, including photocopying and recording, whether electronic or mechanical, now known or hereinafter invented without permission in writing from the publisher.

Dorrance Publishing Co
585 Alpha Drive
Suite 103
Pittsburgh, PA 15238
Visit our website at www.dorrancebookstore.com

ISBN: 978-1-4809-5326-0
eISBN: 978-1-4809-5302-4

Chapter 1

⊷⧫⊶

Getting There

The Texas sky was a glorious blue with shrouds of white puffy clouds before Ponder broke it to pieces, washing the whisker stubbles from his straight razor. He strapped it on the inside of the girth strap on his saddle before using it to remove a couple of days' worth of unattended whiskers on his face and neck. He could feel the sharp blade engage nearly every whisker as it moved slowly across the surface of his skin, making a light click as the blade cut each hair.

The water in the Guadalupe was steady-moving and cool today. Before shaving, he stripped off all but what God gave him and waded into the river just short of knee deep. He sat on the bottom of the river letting the cool water wash away the first three layers or so of filth that covered him. Using his bandana, he scrubbed his body and washed his ears as best he could. A bar of his Mom's soap would be nice right now, but Mom was departed and that was not just a long time ago, but far, far away. He had no soap today, just clear, clean running water and lots of it. He washed his britches, shirt, long johns, and coat as best he could and hung them to dry on a limb outstretched over the river. The socks were worn to near nothing and wet, they resembled a part of the innards of a hog, so they were thrown onto the bank instead of the river so that no one would see them drift by. The bandana was added to the laundry, clothing the limb with the other articles.

With the cleaning done, Ponder gathered the granite coffee pot he carried in his saddle bag, walked to the river bank and caught up some water. He swished it around the inside of the pot and removed whatever might be inside.

1

Then he gathered up a fresh potful, walked to his saddlebag again, and groped around in it until he found the little cotton bag containing some dry beans. After adding a couple of handfuls of the dry beans to the water in the coffee pot, he found the waxy paper that held some dried venison jerky, broke a piece or two off, and placed that with the rest in the coffee pot. After gathering a few pieces of wood and debris from the ground around him, he shuffled a couple of rocks into a circle and placed the fire fuel between the rocks. A flint and striker provided the ignition for the dry fire stuff to begin to smolder and burn. With that, he placed the coffee pot across two close rocks surrounding the fire and let it begin to heat, boil, and cook his paltry meal, some boiled beans.

With a meal started, Ponder gathered his saddle bags and blanket, smoothing the blanket out next to his saddle. He sat and laid back on the blanket while admiring the blue sky above him. With all that, he could slightly smell the small amount of steam coming from his supper cooking in the coffee pot. The sound of Lilly's hoofs shifting her weight while browsing the nearby bushes comforted him and he fell asleep.

Chapter 2

⊷⊜⊜⊷

Wake-up Call

It must have been about the 2nd click of the revolver cocking that awakened him. Laying there on his blanket with his hat over his eyes made him feel a bit vulnerable. The 3rd click premised him to raise his arm slowly and raise the brim of his hat to see who it might be that was cocking the Colt. The barrel of the Colt was about three feet from his head and, seeing the bearer of it, he took the tab of his blanket and attempted to cover more of himself. With two hands, the manipulator of the Colt was aiming it at him. The hands of the person holding the Colt were attached to the most beautiful creature he had ever seen. Looking at her for a moment, he could ascertain that she was very frightened. In looking at the Colt, he could tell that it was his. This beautiful creature had obviously removed the revolver from his saddle bag. He knew that unless she chose to slam the barrel of his Colt down on his head and knock him out, he was fairly safe from getting shot with his own revolver.

As politely as possible he said, "Miss, if you are really wanting to shoot me, you better get the rifle from the scabbard cause I ain't had no balls for that Colt since leavin' Austin".

With that, the woman pulled the trigger only to hear the hammer fall on a dead cylinder. Since Ponder was closer to the rifle than she was, the lady knew that she was no longer a threat. She fell to her knees and began to sob a bit.

"How about I get some clothes on, warm the beans back up, and we share them?" said Ponder.

He arose and covered his nakedness as best he could. He went to the bushes that had been holding his clothes to dry and, with back turned to the woman, got dressed. All the while, he glanced occasionally at this beautiful creature on her knees, still holding the empty Colt with two hands and the end of the barrel resting in the dirt in front of her. He walked to the coffee pot and felt to see if it was warm. He then went to his trappings and retrieved a tin cup, gathered a bit of water from the river, and walked back to the coffee pot. He poured a small amount of the water in the pot and swished the beans. He then rebuilt a small fire like the one the night before and started the warming the beans.

"In a bit we'll have a bite to eat," he said in a low voice, as if not to anyone in particular. Then added, "Don't you want to clean up a bit before you have a bite of these beans I'm fixin'?"

"Hell, I guess so," was the response. Tossing the empty Colt onto Ponders blanket, she stood and began to unbutton her dress, turning and walking towards the river. In just a moment, the woman was naked with her clothes in one hand and stepped into the river. Besides the shapely backside of this gal, he couldn't help but notice the red streaks crossing her back at about shoulder blade height.

Ponder picked up the blanket and shook it a bit. He walked to the bushes by the river and laid it across them, thinking that this woman might want to cover herself once she finished her laundry and scrubbed her body. He also tossed his kerchief to her, thinking she might need something to help remove the dirt from herself. He tossed it and she fully extended her body from the river to catch it, thanking him as she snatched the kerchief and once again immersed herself in the Guadalupe.

"Lord have mercy," Ponder said under his breath as she did this.

By and by, a wet woman stood shaking her hair from side to side ridding it of water. Casually, she waded though the water to the bush where the blanket hanged. Carefully, she placed her wet clothing across the bushes top, stepped onto the bank, and wrapped the blanket Ponder provided around her torso.

Chapter 3

Supper on the Guadalupe

As she walked toward Ponder and the small fire, Ponder exclaimed that supper was ready. He had gathered the only eating implement that he owned, a wooden spoon, from his saddle bag. With spoon in hand he watched this magnificent creature walk to the small fire and sit down on a rock that Ponder had rolled up to the fire as a sitting place.

As she did so, she asked, "Who are you Mister?"

"Ponder," was the simple answer. He picked up the coffee pot with the beans cooked within and said, "Just beans, but they'll get us by."

He handed her the spoon and the pot. She stuck the spoon into the pot, pulled out the spoon laden with boiled beans, took a bite, and chewed them slowly. She had a look on her face that those beans might have been the best thing that she had ever tasted. After a good bunch of beans, she handed the spoon and pot to Ponder who slowly gathered some beans from the pot and put them in his mouth.

"Not too bad," says Ponder, handing the pot and spoon back to the woman.

"I tried to steal your horse, but I couldn't get him to move," said the woman.

"Ain't a him," says Ponder. "Lilly is a she."

The woman nearly choked laughingly exclaiming, "SHE! Lilly! I never heard of a horse named Lilly."

"It was her big brown eyes that made me give her that name," says Ponder. "Kinda made me think of what eyes that Lilly Langtry gal might have. I think she likes it. I gave you my name, what would be yours?" said Ponder.

With that the woman arose and, with blanket still around her, went to the clothes drying bush to check the status of her garments. Reaching them, she lightly laid her hand on parts of her clothes, feeling for any cool dampness. After doing so, it was obvious that her clothes must have been dry, at least to her satisfaction. She turned facing Ponder and allowed the blanket she was wrapped in to fall to the ground at her feet. With this, Ponder nearly lost his breath. The coffee pot with the remaining beans almost fell from his grip. This gal was a breathtaking sight. She had cool, long black hair that was dry by now, big dark eyes set on a slender face, that sat atop the most beautiful body imaginable and she was fairly well-endowed at that. Her eyebrows matched her hair, gracing the brow of her face in slender lines and skin as fair as he had ever seen.

"What would be your name for me, Ponder?" she asked. "Does anything about me make you think of someone or something else?" she added.

Ponder, still perched on the hard rock, was a tad shocked at what had just happened and was quite for a minute while the woman slowly, teasingly, donned her now dry clothing.

"Can I have a few more minutes to consider?" asked Ponder.

In a few minutes, the woman was back to where Ponder sat. She was carrying a grin on her face as she sat back down and asked if there were any beans left in the pot.

"Saving them just for you," said Ponder.

Ponder began to tidy stuff up and get ready to move on before more day was gone. A light chirp of a whistle brought Lilly to where he was standing. He shook the saddle blanket out and placed it across Lilly's back. Then gathered the saddle, brushed a bit of debris from its underside, and gently placed it atop the blanket. Then he stepped to the front of his horse and began to scratch her forehead and rub the sides under her mane, talking gently to her until she threw her head up a bit with a grunt and shook her head at the same time.

"Then I suppose you're ready to go girl," said Ponder.

Gathering his blanket and shaking it out, he swore that he could smell a fragrance about it that must have come from the unknown woman. Next, he carried the coffee pot and spoon to the river's edge where he stooped and rinsed the pot out. There seemed to be nothing to rinse out because it appeared that the woman had retrieved every drop and morsel of what had been cooked in it. But still he washed it as best he could and, with a handful of sand from the river bottom, cleaned the wooden spoon. He walked back to Lilly and, after picking up his saddle bags and lacing them at the rear of the saddle, placed the coffee pot and spoon in the saddle bag. He then retrieved his Henry Repeater from where it was propped against a small tree and inserted it in the scabbard that was already attached to the saddle. As if it was a second thought, he then gathered his canteen, walked back to the river, poured the liquid from it, and stooped to gather fresh water. With that done, all that remained was to bridle Lilly which he did.

All the while, the no-name woman was sitting on the rock by the small, spent fire just whiling away the time.

"You gonna stay here and wait for the next person or are you planning on going with me?" asked Ponder with his back to the woman.

"To be honest Ponder, I was hoping that I could go with you if you would allow it and if Lilly would permit it," was the woman's reply.

Ponder once again walked to the front of Lilly, stroked her forehead, and said, "Lilly gal, would you mind another passenger or would that be too much to ask?"

Lilly turned her head toward the woman as if to judge her, then back to get another head scratch.

"I will take that as an 'okay' by Lilly," replied Ponder.

He stepped into the saddle, hearing all the creaks that leather makes when it gets moved and stretched. The held his hand out toward the woman indicating for her to come on, which she did. She arose from the rock and, smiling, stepped to Lilly's side where Ponder took her hand and swung her aboard behind him.

Chapter 4

⊷⊱⊙ ⊜⊰⊶

Lament Number One — We're Off

Along they went in silence. Ponder still wondering how it came to be that this beautiful woman who was obviously willing to shoot him, displayed her nakedness fully to him, and ate more than half of a meal is now astride Lilly, headed to where she knows not. The marks on her back were still a quandary to him.

He guessed that possibly the luckiest time of this life was having an empty six shooter. Ponder was remembering that he had left his unit in Arkansas with his friend Walt when they got word that Lee had surrendered. The final months of the Confederacy had been very trying because they spent most of the time evading the Northern Army and normally did not have the means to meet them in battle. Both he and Walt left with their horses, weapons, and very little else and made it slowly toward the Texas Coast. It was known that there were still many a head of Longhorns moving wild in the mesquite and salt grass of the lower Texas coast. Their hopes were that there were enough of those wild cattle left to be herded and driven to market somewhere north of Texas to gain a grubstake to begin a life once more.

Once reaching the coast, they spent several weeks surveying their possibilities. There was indeed still an abundant number of the rangy Longhorns about. Scattered in thickets and grasses that clouds of mosquitoes would rise from when riding though the marshy areas. They learned from several people in the area, of Mexican or Indian decent, of various plants that when rubbed on exposed parts of their bodies would temporarily ward off the tiny, pesky, irritating mosquitoes. After surveying what was about, they began building crude corrals in which they might hold these wild Longhorn creatures.

Thus, they began to round the wild cattle one by one and feverishly fight them in the effort to place them in the crude corrals they had constructed of tree limbs and other prevalent vegetation. In a couple of weeks, they had gathered and penned about seventy-five Longhorns. Although they had no currency of any kind, they decided to attempt to hire some help from men they had seen passing through the area. It was going to have to be a pay on delivery situation so they both realized that a greater percentage of any profits from their venture would have to be promised and shook on before any fool would be willing to struggle with the venture ahead. They would move what cattle they could take in and drive them to a market in Kansas or Missouri.

Surprisingly, nine men listened to the plan and, having nothing more promising, shook hands as an agreement to join the fray. Early on, Walt had swapped a rifle, some balls, powder, and a pocket watch that had a small locket attached that once had held a photograph of his now deceased wife to an old Mexican that had a cart that he pulled with a donkey. The old Mexican agreed to gather forage and water to feed the now captured and penned Longhorns. Walt and Ponder both were amazed at how quickly the wild things calmed after being penned and fed. With about six weeks, they had enough critters to total three hundred and thirty. After a short meeting with all who were involved in the venture, it was determined that by noon the next day they would try to have the captured herd of rangy Longhorns move towards a trail that would take them North.

They also discussed the food situation while underway with the herd. Walt suggested that since no chuck wagon was to be had, nor a cook, that each man in turn would provide two meals a day. Each morning the next man in line would ride ahead of the herd and look for a destination to stop the cattle each evening. That man would gather whatever was available and prepare a meal for the men driving the herd towards him. It also was mentioned that the forager for the day would carry what pots and pans they had with him. Also, that on the day he cooked and scouted he would not stand watch at night. This was told to the nine men plus Ponder and a vote was offered if they wished. The few men thought that they would rather cook every ten days than have another share to be taken from the sale of the cattle. The vote was unanimously in favor of Walt's suggestion and so it was. There were some fairly interesting meals fixed on that trip.

Chapter 5

⊷⇒◯⇐⊶

Sit a Spell

Now, here was this beautiful gal on the horse's rump behind him. They had made about twelve miles this morning. They came to a shady thicket near a small stream of moving water, he mentioned to whoever the gal was that they were going to get down for a spell. Having not had much company for a great while, the warmth of the body mounted behind him, the essence of her smell, and the occasional deep breaths she took were pleasing to him. He turned in the saddle a bit, offered his left hand, and helped her dismount from Lilly. When she did so and she was sure-footed on the ground, she straightened her dress out and was looked up at him. She didn't frown or smile, just gave a questioning gaze with her head turned slightly.

Ponder gently turned Lilly a quarter turn and stepped from her back. Then he stood in front of her, rubbed her forehead, and removed her bridle. He stepped to her side and unleashed the girth that held the saddle and stripped it from her back along with the trappings tied to it. Then, with a gentle slap to Lilly's rump, she moved off to the stream to get a drink before foraging in the wild grass and leaves of nearby bushes. She was a good horse and a great friend as well.

Ponder walked to the stream, bent over, cupped a handful of water, and brought to his mouth.

"Good water," said Ponder.

He noticed just along the bank a flat, thin piece of what looked like slate. He then stood and stretched a bit to get the saddle kinks from his body and walked to his pile of trappings to retrieve his Henry from its scabbard. He pulled the lever down just far enough to see if a cartridge was in the chamber and then brought the lever back up.

"Oh my God," said the woman, "You're going shoot me!"

Ponder laughed lightly and said, "Nope, but I'm gonna walk around and see if some critter will jump in front of a bullet, cause my beans have been gone for several hours."

"Whew," said the woman. "I thought that I had overstayed my welcome."

"Nah," said Ponder, "I hardly ever shoot someone until I've known them a bit. Maybe later after we've eaten something. Besides, nobody should meet their maker on an empty stomach."

With that, he took off at a common pace quietly down the creek, the rifle over his shoulder. Surely some creature this late in the day was testing the water as he had. And so, no more than one hundred and twenty-five yards downstream, a yearling deer was keenly sipping water from the creek. He pulled the rifle from over his left shoulder where he was carrying it with his right hand. He slowly, instinctively, pulled the hammer back to where it locked, raised the rifle, and in the same movement pulled the trigger. The young deer fell suddenly to its side and was instantly dead. The sound of the .44 made a light echo through the rocky creek by which Ponder stood. The woman back where he had walked from was caught off guard by the report and was startled for a moment. Ponder pulled the deer carcass back away from the stream and into the bushes where he very quickly dressed and skinned the young deer. It seemed like deer in this area are not very large. Picking the remains up to carry back to camp was much like picking up a laden valise to be carried. He walked back to what was camp for the night with meat.

The short yardage from camp to where the deer was killed was covered quickly by foot. With a piece of rope from his plunder, Ponder hung the carcass on a limb of a cedar.

"Wow," said the woman, "You made short work of that. What can I do to help?"

"Let's find some deadfall and some kindling and get a fire up. Try not to get any cedar, don't want to cook with cedar," Ponder responded.

So they both went about, gathering fire wood. As a small pile of fuel was gathered, Ponder found a couple of green limbs with forks and some rocks. He stood the forked limbs with forked ends up and steadied them with a mess of rocks from the camp area. Then, with some tinder, started a smoky fire with a flint and his knife. He told the woman to add some larger pieces of wood as the fire grew. He walked to the creek and washed his knife blade off then returned back to his trappings and retrieved his canteen. Using the water from the canteen, he washed off the top of a large flat rock near the fire. Then he went over to the deer hanging in the cedar tree. Ponder cut some thin strips of meat from a rear quarter of the deer with his knife, washed them with in the creek, and then laid them on the wetted rock.

Chapter 6

⊷⊜ ⊜⊶

Supper is On

Ponder placed more wood on the small but growing fire. Then he returned to the creek and gathered a thin slab of what appeared to be shale and recovered it from the rocky creek. He wiped it well to remove any debris on it. He went back to the fire then with the flat rock where he laid it in the middle of the embers. He then gathered the strips of venison and laced the plate of slate with the venison strips. Then he went to his saddle and trappings where he retrieved a small coil of heavy wire from a saddle bag and a small cloth sack containing a bit of salt. From the deer carcass, he cut more strips of venison. This time very thin strips, thirty or forty of them. He laid the new pieces out on the once wet rock and sprinkled a bit of the salt from his bag into his hand and coated the thin strips as best he could with the salt crystals.

Taking the coiled wire, he uncoiled it slightly and strung the pieces of salted venison on the wire closely together. Then he carried the string of venison strips to the fire where he hooked each end of the wire on one of the forked sticks that he had previously put in place. They hung high enough for a bit of heat and smoke, but not so close to burn.

Turning to the woman he exclaimed, "Our supper is on. We're gonna get some supper after all. Maybe even something to get us by tomorrow."

The woman had been watching Ponder move around since they arrived at the stream. She was amazed at how he thought everything out so quickly and seemed to get everything in order so naturally. She was also amazed at just the man, the perfect gentleman it seemed. He was the first man she had ever been around that had not pawed at her and she thought that she had suffi-ciently offered the bait for such behavior.

"Ponder," she said, "Is that a first or last name?"

"Either or both," he answered, standing up beside the small fire where supper was being cooked. "I really don't know the answer to that question. My folks died when I was really young and the people that took me in just called me Ponder. So far it's worked pretty well just being plain Ponder."

With that, Ponder recalled that the folks that took him, as well as several other boys who had lost their folks in the influenza epidemic that year. They were not really looking for children as much as hands. All of the adopted hands lived on bunks in the barn. They were fed well and treated decently, but there was no affection shown at all. The kids missed all that. But, the outcome was better than being on their own, which was tough for a kid. The world was not all that kind to children, then or now. He had been working in a field when he heard the sound of gunfire and saw smoke coming from the area where the barn and the house was. He dropped the hoe he was using to clean weeds from between the rows of corn and took off at a fast pace to see what had happened. About halfway there, he could see soldiers on horseback riding away from the home.

Yankee cavalry had killed all the stock around the barn, plus the other two boys that had been taken in. They had also shot Frederick Wheatley and his wife Estell, the couple that had taken him and the other two boys in, to death. All of the structures had been set on fire. Late the next afternoon, young as he was, he became a Confederate soldier. Ponder didn't know what the problem between the states really was, but anyone would do what he did after what he had witnessed the previous day. They needed to be put down and he was as-suredly ready to aid in making that happen. He was 15 years old. For the next couple of years, killing soldiers in blue uniforms became a craft for Ponder. He always hoped that some of the ones that he served their last breath to were some of the ones that had killed the innocent couple on a Missouri farm that day.

While the Wheatley's were not exactly the motherly and fatherly people that his folks had been, they still took him in and treated him decently while no one else had even offered. It was with that Rebel outfit that he had met and became friends with Walt. Walt's fortune had been much like his, the differ-ence being that Walt had run toward the sound of gunfire and a fiery house to find his wife of six months lying dead of gunshot wounds. He too had a yearn-ing hatred of Yankee soldiers. Walt had never involved himself in any way in the war of aggression. Nor had his wife. All they were doing was enjoying their marriage and working like the devil to provide for themselves. They repaid themselves for the hard work put forth and the hardships of starting out with dreams about a big family. That dream was snuffed in a few moments by a group of cruel, hard, and cowardly sons of bitches.

Now, the woman was busying herself at the fire and seemed to be in deep thought. She was moving the cooked slices of venison around on the hot piece of slate. Ponder still did not know what to call her since she had never offered her name. She had asked him what her name should be after the Lilly tale. He had thought about that. She exclaimed that the meat was nearly done. Ponder figured the smell of meat cooking had made him realize how hungry he was. The few handfuls of beans he and the woman shared that morning were absolutely used up. He figured the woman was equally hungry as he. Taking his knife, he fashioned some makeshift forks out of some small limbs he cut from a bush nearby. He scraped all of the bark from them with the knife and, with a handful of sand he picked up, rubbed the homemade forks until no sap showed on them. He then swished them in the creek until they looked clean.

Walking to the fire, he said, "Let's see what we have here."

The woman replied, "As good as it smells, it is bound to be good to eat. Gosh sakes, I'm hungry."

Ponder squatted on the rock by the fire and stretched his legs out. Then he took his knife and rolled the pieces of venison over to see if they were done. They were juicy pieces of meat, cooked slow enough that they did not get tough. Taking his knife, he sliced a few pieces into smaller quarters then handed one of the pieces of cutlery to the woman.

"Give it a try," Ponder said.

Ponders eyes caught the woman's and she had a smile on her face as she accepted the new utensil from him.

From the woman came a sweet, "Thank you very much."

She picked up one of the pieces of venison from the slate and brought it to her lips with her other hand beneath the food so as not to drip the juices on her dress.

She chewed the meat slowly and said, "My god, this is the best thing I ever ate. It is so tender I don't even have to chew it much."

With that, Ponder stuck a piece of the venison with the knife and put it in his mouth and, for a fact, it was good. He glanced at the pieces he was drying on the wire above the fire. He saw that they were drying nicely and had begun to shrink a bit. Several more hours of the low heat and smoke and they will be ready to remove from the wire and stored in a waxed paper sheet he carried for such a reason.

With about four full strips of the cooked venison pieces consumed, the woman reached across and poked Ponder in the ribs saying, "Have you come up with a name for me yet?"

Ponder replied after a moment, "Purty, but I'd hate for you to go through life having to answer to that. The name Canyon might be appropriate because you eat like you trying to fill one. I'm still thinking, give me some time."

He noticed that what he had said seemed to embarrass the woman because her face reddened a bit and she moved her gaze to elsewhere rather than look at Ponder.

"What could be wrong with the name you were given Lady? Are you running from the law or something?" Ponder asked.

Her eyes lifted and looked into Ponder's eyes, saying rather softly, "I'm really not sure, but maybe just as bad."

"Want to tell me about it Purty?" said Ponder with a serious tone. "I certainly don't mind you tagging along and you have only tried to kill me once. So for now we're good I guess. But if we are to spend much more time together, it might behoove you to let me know about something that might come up in the future."

They were still sitting on the rocks, eating cut pieces of the venison. It was silent for a bit.

Chapter 7

⇥━◉ ❖━⇤

Lament Number Two, Knowest All

"One more bite and I will burst," said the woman.

She slowly stood, placed the flats of her hands on her stomach and pushed it in. She turned and moved slowly to the creek where she bent, rinsed her hands and around her mouth, and finally cupped a bit of water and drank it. Ponder's gaze followed her to the stream. The woman's clothing, while it fully covered her, was very plain. Her hair, although not tamed of late by a comb, was still becoming. While not having any make up, on as a lot of women do, it was evident that she needed none. She seemed to be fairly well spoken, but seemed leery about conversation. He also had decided that Purty was not a name she wanted to carry from this camp. Her eyes snapped when he had called her that name. But my goodness she was, in fact, Purty. She was slim of build, but filled the poor dress she wore as well as any woman ever would.

Ponder recalled that the job of driving the cattle North was fairly uneventful. Along the way, they picked up another thirty-three head of cattle. Three hundred and sixty-three head were quite a chore for eleven men. Five head were all they lost in the drive due to encounters with a couple of rivers and broken legs from prairie dog holes. Jacob, one of the nine men that agreed to the proposition, broke his neck when he ran under a big tree near the Red River. It was sad, but no one knew much about Jacob. As a matter of fact, he and Walt were the only two that knew anything at all about the other. Ponder and Walt spoke occasionally about what they might do with Jacobs's share of the sale when they reached Sedalia. It seemed a shame that they didn't have any idea of someone they might send Jacob's share to, which would be the right thing to do on Jacob's behalf. But no one knew anything or anyone connected with Jacob. This was common, men that had left the armies of the North and South simply moved to outer reaches of the country. Sedalia was wild. It was full of wild people. Men in suits and women with too much paint tried their best to work their way into the belt of every new arrival. The cattle were counted and herded into pens and the buyers of them were on the fences looking at the animals coming in to judge them for their worth. Ponder and Walt's herd had enjoyed plenty of water and good grazing the entire trip. The wildness was gone from the longhorns and they looked fat, happy and proud to display themselves while being driven into the Sedalia pens.

Quickly, Ponder was approached by a Chicago buyer. His offer was $19.75 per head on hoof. Ponder had not a clue as to what the market was for the beef. Removing his hat, he slid the kerchief from his neck and wiped the sweat from his head, stuck the kerchief in the waist of his britches, and replaced his hat. In that short a time, another buyer approached and offered $26.40 per head. The first buyer pulled his hat from his head, slapped his leg with it, and walked away.

"Mister, how much will that be for three hundred and sixty-three head?" The buyer said quickly, taking a pencil from over his ear and a piece of paper from his vest pocket.

"Sir, that would be nine thousand five hundred eighty-three dollars and twenty cents."

Ponder never knew that there was that much money in world, much less in Sedalia, Kansas.

"How do you pay that sir?" asked Ponder of the buyer.

"That would be in US dollars sir," answered the buyer. "But just to warn you, if I were you I would get paid at the bank and forward the money somewhere. Walking around Sedalia with that much money might shorten your life a bit."

Ponder and the buyer shook on the deal. It was agreed that Ponder, Walt, and the other eight remaining cowboys would meet at the Merchants Bank in Sedalia and payment would be made there for the cattle to each member of the crew. The deal that he and Walt made with the other drovers was that he and Walt would split half of the amount and the other drovers would share what was left. With Jacob gone, that would be an eight-way split instead of nine. That meant that he and Walt would each take $2395.80 and each of the eight remaining drovers would take $598.95. Not a bad take for a couple of months work.

Ponders thoughts then went to the woman that was walking slowly back to the rock by the small fire.

The woman sat and gathered Ponders' eyes with hers and said softly, "I guess that Purty has been a problem for me for a lot of my life Ponder. I matured rather early in life and I have had a lot of men approach me for favors, you might say. None of these did I accept. My folks lived outside of Nacogdoches. Pa was a farmer and raised a few head of cattle, you know, plain old folks.

"The church we attended had a new preacher show up. He was an unmarried man and in time Albert, that was his name Albert Singley, properly approached me and gained approval from my Pa to court me. He was a handsome man and, although he was a preacher, was extremely exciting to be around. Albert asked for my hand in marriage and it was given. In a short time we were married. I was looking forward to having some children, having a decent husband, and spending the rest of my life with him. Albert seemed hesitant to rush into fatherhood and required me to take precautions from getting pregnant, which I did. As time went by, Albert's time spent away from home during the week increased considerably. According to him, he was visiting folks too far from town to attend church to assure that the word of God was extended to them, no matter the circumstance. It turned out that the spreading the word of God thing was a ruse for playing poker.

"I later figured out that although Albert truly had a love of gambling, he was poor at it. Sometimes the fact that he was a preacher allowed his losses to become somewhat forgivable to those he lost money to, but not always. He returned from a three day 'disappearance' we will call it and he seemed a bit nervous and edgy. My Albert had been in a big card game and lost more money than he had on him, a lot more than he ever would have on him. The bit about being a poor preacher drew no sympathy from the man to whom he owed the debt. Albert had a few bruises on his face and his lip was swollen. I had little sympathy for him because nearly all that he had told me since meeting him seemed to be a fabricated lie. He shakily told me that he was in big trouble, which was obvious by his looks.

"'I've got to do something to pay this debt or I am certain he will come here and kill me,' said Albert.

21

"'Well Albert,' I said, 'What do you propose that you can do to pay the man off?'

"He said, 'I was thinking that you might be able to settle my debt by offering to sleep with him. It might save my life.'

"I was shocked beyond belief. I slapped Albert so hard I knocked him to the floor, calling him a sorry son of a bitch. Albert responded by grabbing his razor strop, throwing me across our bed, and lashing my back with it several times. I was hurt, angry, and frightened, but mostly angry.

"'Albert said, 'Why don't you fix me some supper? Let's get some sleep and you just think about it. It would be a one-time deal, so you would never have to do such thing ever again. Just think about it, that's all I ask.'"

"I did fix him some supper," she said. "I washed to go to bed as it was late. The hurt was welling inside me and my back hurt badly from the whipping."

She then said that a bit later after she had gone to bed, Albert came to bed also and, without a word or apology, simply rolled over and went to sleep.

"I got up to get a drink of water and noticed one of my knives lying on the counter. I picked up the knife and, handling it, somehow my hurt became changed to full anger. I went to the bed, rolled my sleepy Albert onto his back, and cut him from asshole to appetite with that knife. Then I gathered my few belongings and left on foot. Ten days later I came upon your camp."

"Well we are not going to call you Purty and that is a fact lady," said Ponder.

Ponder had never met Albert but laid no blame on this woman for what she had done. Had he known Albert and found out what the man had done to this woman, his wife or any other woman, he would have cut him too and probably fed him to the hogs if any were about.

The woman sat on the rock with her face in hands. Telling Ponder the story of her problem had both embarrassed and frightened her as she had no idea what he would think of what had happened. He may be a man that would expect his wife to give sex in payment of a gambling debt like Albert had. She prayed that he was not.

Chapter 8

⋅►═╕ ╘═◄⋅

Relieving the Bounty

Back in Sedalia, all eleven members of Ponder and Walt's crew had arrived at the Merchants Bank as planned. Ponder and Walt went in the bank manager's office with Mr. Claxton, the Chicago Cattle buyer. Papers were signed to move the herd to the buyer's ownership. In a bit, the bank manager left the room and returned with the agreed amount in cash. He laid it out in counted stacks on the top of his oaken desk. Walt stepped from the room and asked the other nine drovers to come into the office, which they did. With this, Mr. Claxton shook Ponder's hand, tipped his hat to Walt and the other nine drovers, and left the room.

Ponder told the bank manager the agreement they had on payment to each man and asked the bank manager if he might count those amounts out to each of them from the stack. The Bank Manager obliged and left the room after having done that. Ponder conveyed what Mr. Claxton had told him about the safety of men that might be carrying money in Sedalia and gave them the choice of what they wanted to do after leaving that office. The discussion between them was short and all except Ponder just wanted to boot their money and, after a hot bath and meal cooked by someone else, consumed at a table with a chair, skedaddle out of Sedalia. Ponder had planned to wire all but fifty dollars of his share to a bank in Fredericksburg, Texas but the Sedalia Bank was not able to communicate with the Texas Bank. So Ponder booted his money just as the others had done.

Chapter 9

⊷⟝◯ ◯⟞⊶

Parting Ways

The nine hands left as one but after a drink in the nearest saloon, they were back on the street, patting one another on the back, pointing fingers at each other and laughing. They soon mounted their saddled horses and left Sedalia in several different directions. It wasn't long before pairs of them were no longer, just one man aboard a horse headed to God knows where. Ponder knew very little about any of them. They came and they went. None spoke much about who they were, where they came from, or where they were headed. In his mind, he wished them well. They had been good men to be around and he had nothing bad to say about any one of them. Turning to Walt, Ponder asked him what plans he might have.

"I just don't know Ponder," he responded. "Don't have anything to go back to or anything of mine to fetch." He looked away. "I suppose I need to go find something to call mine, where ever that may be. It might be someplace in hell, I don't know. But I guess I'll go looking for it just the same."

With that, both men extended their hands and a slow handshake ensued, both looking into the eyes of the other, for they had been down a long path together. Walt did not drink any liquor, so Ponder had not even suggested that they have a farewell drink, but he decided to step into a saloon and indulge himself in at least one drink of whiskey.

With his thoughts coming back to the present, Ponder noticed that the woman had been sitting on the rock with her face in her hands.

Ponder queried softly, "Are you alright?"

Slowly, her face rose from her hands and tears were running down her face. She outstretched her arms.

She was sobbing but asked, "What in the world am I going to do? I have killed my husband and ran away. Most likely there are people looking to find me. I have nothing but these clothes on my back and what God gave me. I cannot care for myself – hell I can't even shoot a gun right or tell if it's loaded. Were it not for a man that I don't know from Adam I would have starved to death. I can't even take care of myself."

Ponder said nothing for a bit. He felt sorry for this poor gal. She was raised in a home that had people in it that loved her and then hooked up with the scum of the earth man, he was reluctant to classify her ex-husband as a man. Then she ends up in the middle of Texas unaware of how to survive in the elements. He was almost glad that she was willing to shoot him. That showed that she at least had some grit about her.

Ponder finally replied, "Lady, we are going to get you a name, rest assured we will do that, and whether you believe it or not after all you have been through of late you are going to be okay. We are going to move slowly the next few days and talk, if you wish. Enough to get all of this spent from your mind. But, after all you have experienced of late, why did you expose yourself to me by the river as you did? Had it been a lot of men I've known, you might have had to deal with that."

"I had to do that Ponder," said the woman. "I wanted to see your reaction so I would know whether I should start getting away really quick or just wait and see who and what you are. It seems that I have lucked out because I've not had to run or fight you off. Also Ponder, thanks for being kind to me."

She stood up, stooped, and put her arms around Ponder with him sitting on his rock and she kissed him on his forehead.

Ponder was rather shocked, but stood and made do over the meat drying on the wire above the small smoky fire.

"Kathryn," he said, "You might gather some small chunks of limbs and place them on the coals of the fire. The meat needs a bit more heat and time to be fit for tomorrow."

Without any comment, the woman walked away from what was camp and gathered some pieces as Ponder had asked her to do. She returned to the fire and was placing the wood pieces atop the coals when it dawned on her what

Ponder had called her. She stood and turned slowly to Ponder and with her head turned slightly to the side.

With a grin on her face, she said, "How did you know that was my name, Ponder?"

Ponder replied softly that Kathryn had been his mother's name and that, in talking to Lilly about it, decided that it was a suitable name for her. Kathryn beamed.

Ponder then said, "We might call you Kat for short. Would you mind that?"

"Of course not Ponder. I've always liked to called that by people I like."

Then Ponder recalled Walt's fate.

From the end of the street he stood on in Sedalia, Ponder saw Walt, at the other end, step out of a mercantile store with some packages. Ponder was sure they were provisions that he would need in his travels from here. Walt had just tied the provisions across the trappings laced on to the saddle's rear skirt when he heard a pop. Though the street was busy and it was far away, Ponder knew for certain the noise was gunfire. He saw Walt lean quickly to his left and fall onto his back in the dirt street. He could see Walt's hand reaching down and bringing his Colt up and in a split second Walt fired once, twice, and a third time. From a place that Ponder could not see the figure of a man, with a six gun dangling in his right hand, fell onto the board-walk in front of the store that Walt had come from. Ponder broke into a run and in a moment was alongside Walt, who by this time was flat on his back in the dirty street.

Walt's right hand clutched the Navy Colt he carried and that had sent the man on the boardwalk to meet his maker. Walt's arm was motionless and was lying along his right side. The moment Ponder got on his knees next to Walt he could see a pool of very dark red blood gathering under Walt's back right side about hip level.

Walt's eyes slowly caught Ponders and he said, "It's been good Ponder." He paused. "My Kathryn…"

A stillness came to his eyes, and he was gone.

Ponder sat cross-legged next to Walt for a while, looking at him and think-ing about where they had been and what they seen and done. Ponder noticed that a small crowd had gathered. Men in filthy clothes that smelled like sa-loons, men in suits that looked like they were going to try to sell him some-thing, and a few women who stood with a hand over their mouth as if they could not believe what they were seeing. Ponder slowly stood up, dusted himself off, and pointed down the street where his Lilly was.

"See that horse down there looking this way? I'm gonna walk down there, bring her here, and gather my friend up. I'm gonna take him from this god forsaken place and bury him. When I start this direction, if there is a person within thirty feet of my friend, I am going to pull my Henry Rifle out and commence killing all that are there."

Ponder walked away to get Lilly. He took her reins and turned back towards Walt. He noted that no one was within thirty feet of where Walt lay. In fact, he could not see another human on that end of the town.

What memories he had, but now the woman, Kathryn, seemed to be a different person since Ponder told her what her name was. She was wearing a smile and seemed to be a bit more at ease than when she first arrived. The sun was beginning to set and shades of red, orange, and blue were draping the skyline to the west. Ponder checked the strips of venison hanging over their small fire and determined that the strips were as dry as they were ever going to get. He took an end of the wire in each hand and lifted the rack of dried venison from above the fire. Hooking the two ends of wire together, he hung the meat on the limb of a cedar not far away. He then went about picking up some larger pieces of dead, dry wood and placed them on the fire to provide a bit of light when darkness finally fell.

Lilly was lolling about at the edge of camp grazing on some grasses and leaf ends on the various trees and bushes, raising her nose and snorting now and then. Kathryn took up the saddle blanket and shook it fiercely, removing what debris that she could from it. She unrolled the blanket roll from Ponder's saddle which was propped up on the ground. She shook it just as she had done the saddle blanket. She folded it in quarters and then placed it on a tree limb as she had the saddle blanket. Ponder liked seeing her casually flit around doing stuff. He had never had much company in his travels, except for Walt. Walt spoke few words and most times they both just went about doing for themselves. Having a beautiful woman in camp was an experience he had not ever had before. As a matter of fact, he hadn't had just about any experience with a woman.

Ponder supposed that Kathryn must have gotten some mental relief from being able to tell someone what she had been through. She walked with sureness about her, it seemed. Her hair, long, straight, and black as the night, wisps around her face as she moved. It was as if her hair, if it become detached from her scalp, would simply float away. Even the skin on her pale white face seemed to have gained some color.

Then he remembered Walt again, he recalled rising from where he had been sitting alongside Walt's body. He removed his hat and, as he scratched his head, looked toward the mercantile store that was only separated from him by the boardwalk. He placed the hat back on his head, stepped onto the boardwalk, and walked into the store.

The man inside, apparently the owner, said, "Sorry about your friend Mister. Charlie Franks, the man that shot your friend, was standing around in here when your friend gave me the order for the provisions he wanted to buy. When they were all gathered up and wrapped, I told your friend what he owed me. He reached inside his boot and pulled a roll of money. The bill was seven dollars and twenty cents. Your friend counted out the money on the counter and slid it to me. About that time Franks told your friend, 'I'll take a hundred of that purse you rebel trash.'"

The shopkeeper said, "I guess Franks noticed that Leech & Rigdon pistol in your friend's belt and knew he was a Confederate.

"'Ain't gonna happen fella,' said Walt, as he gathered his change and goods and walked towards and out the door of the store.

"'I'm gonna kill that rebel son of a bitch,' Franks said.

"When your friend got outside, Franks stood in the doorway, pulled out his shooter, and shot your friend without saying one word."

Ponder walked to the wall and picked up a shovel, after finding out what it cost, paid the storekeeper and walked out the door to Lilly. He retrieved his Henry rifle from the scabbard where he had placed it and stuck the shovel handle into it, replacing his rifle. He then stepped onto the boardwalk and rolled Charlie Franks over. There were three .36 caliber holes in the forehead of Franks, between his hat line and nose. Ponder hailed a young boy standing near and reached in his pocket and pulled out a one-dollar coin.

Handing the coin to the boy, Ponder said, "Find out where this Charlie Franks' horse is and bring it to me. I want the saddle and bridle too, if it ain't already on the horse."

With that, Ponder stripped Charlie Franks buck naked. Ponder then folded the dead man's clothes, set them beside Franks boots and spurs, and stacked Franks' gun rig and revolver on top of the clothes and then placed

Charlie Franks' hat on top of the whole mess. With that, he returned to the mercantile and bought a piece of canvas about six foot by eight foot. Outside, Ponder tore a thin strip from one edge of the piece of canvas, pulled the Leech and Rigdon from Walt's belt, and stepped back up to where Charlie Franks laid. Ponder sat Franks up against the mercantile wall on the boardwalk and used the strip of canvas to tie the Leech & Rigdon revolver around his neck.

Knowing that no one wanted to be seen with that Confederate pistol, Ponder doubted that anyone would take it. Franks could lay there dead in his altogether until the stink made someone do something about him. Stepping again to the street, Ponder turned and with a short, curt salute while facing Franks.

"Fine outfit ya got there, Yankee." He said.

Ponder rolled the canvas out next to Walt's body, still lying in the dirt street. He then gently rolled Walt onto the canvas and then rolled Walt and the canvas until Walt's body was completely consumed in the canvas. With two more strips pulled from the canvas' edge, Ponder tied each end of the canvas roll shut. He then lifted Walt's canvas covered corpse from where it rested and, getting his shoulder under the roll, placed Walt's remains across the saddle of Walt's horse, which was still tied to the rail in front of the mercantile.

By this time, the boy whom he had given the dollar to retrieve Charlie Franks' horse came walking up, leading the horse. Ponder gathered all that he took from Charlie Franks' dead body and lashed the whole mess to the top of Franks' saddle. He retrieved the Henry from where it leaned, untied the reins of Walt's horse from the rail and, taking Franks' mount's reins, mounted Lilly with the Henry cross his legs and, without as much as a look around, slowly rode south out of Sedalia, trailing both horses alongside. Then Ponders thought came back to the present.

Chapter 10

Falling Stars

It was just short of dark when Kathryn asked Ponder, "Where are we going to sleep tonight?"

Ponder replied after a bit, "I think we'll get back towards those bushes," pointing at some scrub oak about twenty feet from the little fire. "And we might get up under the edge of the bushes to keep the dew off of us in the early hours. Plus, it will make someone have to look around a bit if they somehow smell our little fire. There might be some critters moving tonight, they'd be after that deer carcass. But they won't bother us," Ponder added.

With that, Ponder picked up the saddle blanket and walked to the edge of the scrub oak he had mentioned. He sort of spun the saddle blanket up under the small oak's limbs.

"Kind of like that, Kathryn. Would that suit you?"

Kathryn's response was that if that was what he felt was best, then that's what she wished also. She took the blanket that she had shook out earlier, walked to where he had placed the smaller saddle blanket, and folded it at the foot of it. From Ponders' saddle bag, he retrieved two kerchiefs.

Handing Kathryn one of them, he said, "I'm going to go down the creek a way and wash a bit. All I have are these kerchiefs, but they should work to clean the dust off us." So down the creek in near darkness went Ponder. He could hear Kathryn's footsteps right behind him.

Ponder stopped, turned, and said, "Kathryn, I plan to wash as much of me as I can reach, so you might want to stay up on the end of the creek."

He could see her beautiful face even in near darkness and she said, "Ponder, I would rather be on this end of the creek with you, if you don't mind. I don't think that you are going to see anything that you haven't seen before."

Ponder replied with, "That's up to you Kathryn."

What Kathryn did not realize was that what she had shown of herself that morning was a bit more than Ponder had ever been privy to. While his life's experiences were numerable, his knowledge of a woman was extremely limited. Ponder picked a spot that was covered with flat rocks and a little grass. He stopped there and sat down. He removed his boots and stood to remove his britches, shirt, and suspenders. Then he stepped into the cool water of the little creek. It was hard not to notice that Kathryn had done much the same. Darkness or not, even the stars coming out at nightfall were enough to pretty much display the fullness of Kathryn. Ponder was a bit grateful for the lack of light because he was embarrassed to the fullest extent, certain he was that he was glowing like an ember. Both dipped their kerchiefs in the cool water of the little running creek and began to wash away the dust of the day and the smell of smoke from the little fire they had used. Kathryn acted as if Ponder was not even present. But he was, and he was mortified about what he was seeing and experiencing.

Kathryn quietly said, "This feels wonderful Ponder. This ought to make me sleep sound."

With a light clearing of his throat, Ponder replied, "I hope so."

Kathryn had pretty much cleaned everything. Hell, it would have been difficult to have missed it.

Ponder slipped his britches and boots on, leaving his suspenders hanging from his waist, and walked back to the camp area. He would be dry soon and would slip his shirt on then. Kathryn walked back to the camp area holding her clothes and shoes in her hand. She sat down on the flat rock, brushed the sand from her feet, and then put her shoes on. She sat there for a minute and then stood, placed her dress, which she had folded, onto the flat rock she had been sitting on, walked to the saddle blanket, and laid down after having removed her shoes again and setting them to the side.

"That did feel wonderful," Kathryn said to Ponder.

"Indeed it did Kathryn," said Ponder. "Kathryn, I was supposed to sleep on that saddle blanket tonight. I was going to tell you to use the real blanket."

This beautiful woman was stark naked laying on the saddle blanket. Dark or not, just light from the stars made her totally visible.

"Ponder," Kathryn said sternly, "There is no way you can sleep on this saddle blanket all night without some cover. If you sleep dressed, then stay dressed, get the blanket, lay down here beside me, and cover us up."

"Kat," said Ponder sternly, "I don't sleep dressed."

"Then were you planning to lay on the ground naked and cover yourself with this saddle blanket? Ponder!" said Kathryn. "Get the blanket, undress, lay down here with me, and cover us up."

Ponder was at a complete loss. He had known this woman since just this morning and already he had seen her without clothes a couple of times. Now she wants him to sleep under the same blanket with her, without any clothes either. But, turning his back to Kathryn as best he could, he did take his boots and britches off, lifted the blanket from where he had placed it for Kathryn, stood at the end of the saddle blanket where she now lay, and sat down, pulling the wool blanket over them both. Glancing over at her, he could see the reflection of stars in the Texas sky in her eyes.

"Kathryn?" said Ponder, "Are you accustomed to doing things like this?"

Her reply was, "Nope!"

"Then why now?" asked Ponder.

Kathryn rolled over facing Ponder, she placed her hand softly on the side of his face. She said, "Ponder, I tested you this morning. By this evening I would trust you on anything you do. If you wanted to take me, you could. By now I doubt that I would even fight you. You've been kind, thoughtful, and have listened to the horrors of my life. My day thus far with you is nicer than the past year of my life. I'm sure that you have known a lot of women and to you I am most likely old hat."

Ponder slid from beneath the blanket and retrieved the Henry and laid it beside him, beneath the blanket, just in case.

Ponder led the two horses out of Sedalia. In about four miles he saw a little place where some farmer lived. Past there about a quarter mile was a ridge with cottonwoods running out to the edge of farmed land. Ponder pulled up at the farm house, removed his hat, went to the farmhouse door, and knocked gently. A sunburnt small man opened the door. Next to him was a young boy, equally as sunburnt as the man that opened the door.

"Hello, can I help you?" said the farmer.

"Yes sir, maybe you can," said Ponder. Pointing to the horse with Walt's body aboard, Ponder stated, "That horse is carrying the body of my friend who was shot to death in Sedalia this morning. I am looking for a final place for him, his name was Walt." He pointed at the ridge beyond and the cottonwoods. "I've a mind to bury Walt on the ridge point beneath that stand of cottonwoods if it would not interfere with the owner's business."

The farmer said that he saw no reason for his friend Walt could not lay on that ridge and that it was his land but would never be farmed.

"If that's the case," said Ponder, "I am going to take Walt up there and try to give him a decent burial. I thank you sir and I'll be heading up there."

In a bit, Ponder was on the ridge with Walt across the saddle on his horse and the horse that had belonged to the man that had taken his life. The horses were left untethered to enjoy the grasses on the ridge near him. Ponder stepped from the saddle, with his Henry rifle in his hand, pulled the shovel he purchased at the mercantile from his rifle scabbard and replaced it with the Henry rifle.

With shovel in hand, he walked towards the cottonwoods, surveying the area. He wanted to put Walt to rest facing the East, which was the custom. Finding what he thought was a good spot, he removed his hat, throwing it to the side, and started digging. With the exception of a fist sized rock, the digging was fairly easy as the soil was sandy and loose. In a sideways glance back toward the farmhouse, Ponder could see what appeared to be three people walking towards the ridge where he was digging the grave for Walt. The grave was not completed yet, but Ponder set the shovel aside and went to the horse carrying Walt. He steadied Walt's horse and stepped back to the side, taking Walt from atop his horse onto his shoulder. He carried Walt to the side of the grave where no dirt was piled and gently lay him down. Releasing the tie on the bottom of the piece of canvas that Ponder had sealed, he carefully pulled Walt's boots from his feet and took them several yards away and sat them down. He then reached inside the right boot which is where he knew Walt had held his cattle money. Taking that, he went to where Lilly was grazing, raised the flap on one side of his saddlebag, and deposited Walt's money there.

After rubbing Lilly's head for a minute, he returned to where Walt lay and tied the canvas back together. Ponder had slightly more to dig before the size was satisfactory, so he worked to finish that job.

Noticing that the farmer, his wife, and his child were nearly to the ridge, he waved as a friendly gesture to them. Ponder the cleaned the loose matter from the hole and squared the edges a bit, although there was no coffin to put

Walt away in. Moments later, the three-member family was with him on the ridge at Walt's grave site.

The farmer, removing his hat, extended his hand to Ponder and said, "I'm Bob Wagner." Then, with his hand held toward the woman, said, "This is my wife Mildred" and then gestured toward the boy, "and our son Robert. Mister, we are sorry for your loss. Mildred brought our Bible if you would like something said for your friend."

"Walt," Ponder said. "Mr. Wagner, I'm sure that Walt would be pleased to have you folks here and to have words said over him. I've a bit more to do if you folks want to sit and rest a minute," said Ponder.

The Wagners turned as one and walked to the cottonwoods where they sat down in the grass.

Ponder stepped into the dug grave and, turning towards Walt, ran his arms between the earth and Walt's back, carefully lifting him up and into the top of the grave. Then still just as carefully laid Walt in place.

Standing there in the grave with Walt's remains, Ponder said, "Walt, you have been a good friend. We have seen much together. Maybe Kathryn will find you. You were a good man. Goodbye Walt."

Ponder then stepped out of the grave. He took the shovel from nearby and began shoveling the pile of dirt back into the hole where Walt lay. In a moment, Mr. Wagner was there. He placed his hand on Ponder's shoulder and took the shovel from him. Ponder then stood as Mildred and Robert walked to the graves edge where he stood and joined him. Mr. Wagner placed the fill back into the grave with great care until it was done. When all was done and all four of them stood beside the new grave, Bob Wagner removed his hat and all of them, including Ponder, bowed their heads.

"Lord Almighty," said Bob Wagner, "Take this man, Walt, and carry him under your loving arm to heaven above. Amen."

Just afterwards, Ponder pointed at Walt's horse and told Mr. Wagner, "That was Walt's horse. I am certain that Walt would have wanted you folks to have his horse and saddle for your kindness. Walt was like that, sir. You can keep him or sell him, if you have the mind."

Bob Wagner replied saying how gracious the gesture was and that he would accept the gift from Walt and that they would watch over Walt's grave so long as they could. Ponder turned and, stepping to where Walt's horse stood, took it by the reins and walked it to Mr. Wagner and handed him the reins. Ponder then retrieved his hat from where he had laid it, placed it on his head, boarded Lilly, and took Charlie Franks' horse by its reins. He tipped his hat to the Wagners and bid them farewell.

Chapter 11

Looking for Utopia

Ponder rode off with the extra horse in tow. He rode in the direction of the trail that he and the others brought the cattle up on. It would eventually take him through the east side of the nations and back into the Northeast corner of Texas. Along the way, somewhere in Oklahoma or Arkansas, he came across a trade store and stopped to get some supplies. The goods that Walt had bought just before he was killed had been exhausted for a couple of days now. Some dry beans, coffee, salt pork, some salt and pepper, and a few cans of those peaches he had heard about would fit the bill. If they had them, a box or two of flat Henry 44s and some paper cartridges for the Colt .36 caliber Navy he carried would be good. Dealing at the trade store worked out well for Ponder, they had the cartridges for both his Henry and the Navy Colts as well. Plus, the man that owned the store took the extra horse with saddle, blanket, and bridle. He also took the Colt taken from Charlie Franks, plus it's belt and holster in trade and even gave Ponder forty-five dollars back in the trade.

Ponder loaded his provisions and headed in the direction of Texas. He crossed this area once more, having no problems with Indians or bandits. Even the rivers had been easily crossed. But still, he kept a wary eye. Riding for days at a time alone on horseback made him wish for a little talk that isn't to come and leaves a lot of time for the recollection of past experiences which, except for the trip to Sedalia, were mostly not times he wished to fully remember. He had seen some Indians, four to be exact. They were on horseback and moving slowly. Ponder knew that they had seen him, but they must have been intent on going some special place because they paid him no mind. He had seen several groups of people in laden wagons traveling slowly in a westerly direction. Probably folks striking out to find a new life for themselves. In his mind, he silently wished them well. These were hard times and this part of the country was made up of a lot of people who, just like the times, were hard.

Ponder laid there for a minute considering Kathryn's comment about him knowing a lot of women and her being "old hat". He had not known a lot of women. As a matter of fact, he had known no women in his life to speak of. He had only seen paintings of nude women on the walls in the few saloons he had been in.

There were what they called "camp women" that followed the military units around and offered "special" services to those that had money to pay. He had never had anything to do with that. From the beginning, he had heard of diseases that men might get from a frolic with these camp women. He just stayed out of that. Now here lay this beautiful creature with not a stitch on, right next to him.

"Kathryn," Ponder said, "I am twenty-one years of age. I doubt that you are much over nineteen years. You've been married and all, so there is no doubt that you have had some experience with men. But Kathryn to be honest with you, I don't know anything much about women. I know that you think I am pulling your leg, but the only nude woman that I have ever seen, that wasn't painted on a piece of board or canvas, was you today. I know fully what takes place between a man and woman sometimes, whether or not they are man and wife. But I have no experience in that."

There was silence for a moment, then Kathryn rolled to her left side and put her elbow under her to raise her up. With her right hand she reached and, taking the right side of Ponder's face, turned his face towards hers.

"Ponder," Kathryn said softly, "Were I to be capable of going back in time, it would not have been the clean clothes and nice suit of a man with an education that would have drawn me to marriage, but rather a man as yourself. I am a little shocked of certain experiences that you lack in a world such as we have. But in your case, after one day, I am sad that I settled for what I saw on the outside of a man, rather than what was on the inside of him. Ponder, I am going to lay here beside you just as before. I would enjoy the comfort of having you here beside me under this blanket.

"I'll ask you that if we come to a place where you believe that I can make it on my own and wish to rid yourself of me, I will trust your judgment. You can ride away and I will strike out to make a place for myself, wherever that may be. If you simply wish for me to go, I will even do that. What I truly wish for is to stay with you until you reach where it is you are going."

Ponder had no reply. He knew, for instance, that Kathryn had bathed in the same creek water as he and had washed with a kerchief similar to his, but it certainly seemed that Kathryn had a fragrance about her that was different than his. Kathryn rolled back off her elbow and on her back-side again. She did however seem to leave no room in the distance away that their bodies were.

Ponder was content with what he had told Kathryn about his innocence. He was not ashamed. But had always wished that if he found someone, that they could take pride in being the first for him.

Kathryn said, "and I am nineteen, Ponder."

In a short while, Ponder rolled to his left side and could feel the cool barrel of the Henry Rifle against his leg. A few moments later, an owl in a nearby tree hooted. Kathryn also rolled to her left side and Ponder could feel every bit of her against him. He could even feel the warmth of her breath against his back.

Nine days out of Sedalia and Ponder was on the side of a rocky hill just to the west of Austin, Texas. From where he sat, he could see the buildings that make up the city of Austin. It looked like a busy place. He had reached this point late yesterday and, after a night's sleep, he was up, had a cup of coffee, and enjoyed the final can of peaches he had bought way back in the nations. He talked to Lilly a bit, checked her feet and legs, and rubbed her neck and mane.

In the night, he had taken the cattle money from his boot. It was his and Walt's share of the cattle sale. Next to a bunch of cedars at daylight he had found a very large, heavy piece of limestone. He worked to lift it and leaned it against a fair-sized cedar, by which the rock lay. He used his boot heel to scoop a shallow trench under where the rock did and would lay again. Taking the cattle money, he rolled it up and placed it in the can that had once held the peaches he had as breakfast this morning and placed the can in the small furrow he had made. Ponder then grasped the big stone and placed it back where it had obviously lay for hundreds if not thousands of years. In his boot, he still had some fifty or so dollars from the trade of Charlie Franks' horse, saddle, and Navy Colt at the trading Post.

Chapter 12

‹•─◦ ◦─•›

Recollections of Austin

With the Henry in its scabbard and a Navy Colt at his waist, Ponder swung himself up onto Lilly and headed for Austin. Ponder was hoping to find a hotel to spend a night in a bed, a meal served on a plate with utensils to use, and a long, hot bath. He wanted this fairly close to a livery where Lilly could stay for the night and maybe have something besides grass to eat. It would be a treat for the both.

Down the rocky hill and into Austin they rode. Coming to Congress Street, Ponder could see hoards of people dotting about doing their fare of the day. Men in suits and women dressed well carrying umbrellas were walking in and out of shops and visiting with others doing the same thing. Ponder turned Lilly south on Congress and went several blocks until Ponder saw a small, two story hotel named the Gist Hotel. Just a few doors down there was a sign advertising "Hickham's Livery". It looked made to order. This was obviously not the upscale part of Austin. He could also see red lamps at the upper ends of stairs leading off Congress Street. The street was also wet from privy pots having been emptied by the fluid being thrown from windows. It was a remarkable smelling place.

He first hitched Lilly to the rail in front of the Gist Hotel. Ponder then walked though the bar-room type doors into the small lobby of the hotel. At the registration desk, he rang the little bell to get an attendants attention, which he did. The clerk told him the cost of a room for a night was two dollars and fifty cents and a hot bath was seventy-five cents, with soap it was ninety cents. Ponder counted out four dollars and signed the registry. The clerk grudgingly gave him ten cents change, looking over his wire rim glasses. Ponder told the clerk that as soon as he got his horse stabled, that he would be back for the bath.

"Your room is number three, up the stairs, second room on the right," said the clerk.

Ponder walked out the door, unhitched Lilly, and walked her the few doors down to the livery and inside.

"Help ya?" came a voice from within one of the stalls.

"I need to put my horse up for today and tonight. I'd like to have her brushed and I'd like for her to have some oats or some type of grain if its available."

"Wanna pay now or when you get your horse mister?" said the livery keeper.

"Whatever you prefer, Mr. Hickham is it?"

"Tomorrow. That'd be fine, mister?" said the liverier.

"Ponder is the name."

Ponder gathered his Henry from the scabbard and, reaching into his saddle bag, took a cleaner shirt out than he had on now plus his razor. Walking out of the livery, he noticed a saloon across the street that had a sign in the window that had "restaurant" written on it.

Ponder said to himself, "Looks like I am set for the night."

Walking back to the hotel, Ponder surmised the people in the area of town where he was. They were not the well dressed, busy, friendly people that he had seen on the north end of Congress Street where he had entered Austin. He found the bath facility in the back, outside of the hotel. It was a stone building about fifteen to eighteen feet square with good sized, banded metal tubs sitting in it. A wooden walkway ran from the front door and alongside the individual tubs. A piping from the back wall ran to each tub. Behind the bath was a big boiler with a wood fire beneath it.

Pretty fancy for southside Austin, Ponder thought. A short man with a stooped back came shuffling in and told Ponder that as soon as he got in a tub that he would wash his clothes, if he wished, for fifty cents.

"I can dry them on the boiler outside and that don't take long," said the little man. Ponder found seventy-five cents and placed it in his hand. The man shook the coins in his hand and then placed them in a small bag at his waist. Ponder chose a tub at the rear of the room. He stood his Henry against the corner wall and then pulled his boots off and placed them on the wooden bench. Ponder pulled his Navy from his waist and laid it on the bench. Off came his jacket, shirt, and pants and a tap on his shoulder was that of the little attendant standing with his hands out to get Ponder's dirty clothing.

Ponder then took his hat off and placed it over the Navy on the bench. Over the side of the tub Ponder put a leg into some maybe warm, but certainly not hot, water.

"Give me a minute mister," said the attendant, as he stepped out the door to the boiler. In a moment, the light screech of a valve could be heard and Ponder could feel the warmth of hot water coming through the pipe into the tub. Studying the situation, Ponder could see that another pipe was attached to the tub near the top that served as an overflow. He guessed that the water that ran off must go into a ditch or creek behind the bath house somewhere.

"Let me know if it gets too hot," he heard the attendant say.

The water got warmer quickly and it felt good to Ponder. He immersed himself in the hotter water several times and he could feel the filth sliding from his body. His face had whisker growth on it, but he would shave in his hotel room where he hoped there was a mirror. The attendant walked by, tossing a wash cloth and bar of soap to Ponder. Ponder thought that he had never felt so good in his whole life. The hot water and sweet smelling soap was seemingly relieving the soreness of sitting in a saddle every day for several months and sleeping on hard ground and rocks. He scrubbed his face, ears, neck, belly, knees, feet, toes, between his toes, arm pits, arms, butt, and all that was left and did the same again. He was actually so relaxed that he hoped he would not to have to ask the little man that was the attendant to help him out of the tub once his clothes were washed and had dried. Ponder laughed a bit, think of what the headlines would be if he drowned in the wash tub, "Smiling Man Found Dead Floating in Hot Tub of Water".

It wasn't long before the little man attendant showed up with Ponder's clean, dry, folded clothes and laid them on the bench beside his hat. The man came back shortly and laid a fresh towel on the bench also. Ponder noticed the squeaky valve on the hot water line squeaking again, indicating that the hot water valve was being closed.

Reluctantly, Ponder stood and stepped out of the tub of water onto the wooden walk. He had never felt so limber in his life than he did right now. He figured that he might get used to the hot bath habit. With all of his clothes on and the Navy Colt in his pant waist, hat on his head, spare shirt now clean, and his Henry in hand, he went to find the attendant and gave him another dollar.

"It was worth that mister," he said.

A new man he was or at least he felt he was. Ponder left the bath house, entered the back of the hotel, and went up the stairs to his room. The Henry was stood in the hinge corner of the door and the Navy was tossed onto the bed along with his hat. Walking the few steps to the window in his small room, Ponder looked out onto the street. There was not a lot going on outside except a few more horses at the rail then when he had checked into the Gist Hotel. It was about noon and Ponder decided that he would rest a bit and later would figure out what he would have to eat. Turning the little skeleton key in the lock on the hotel room door, Ponder was thinking that maybe he would go ahead and shave before laying down. He poured some water from the pitcher into a small wash bowl, gathered up his razor from the pocket on his jacket, and began to cut the stubble from his face. It was surprisingly easy to cut after the hot bath. In a short while, after searching his face with his hand for whiskers he missed, he rinsed the razor in the water bowl and returned it to his jacket pocket. Then, taking the towel from atop the table provided in the room, he wiped his face well to dry it and remove any residue from shaving.

Turning towards the window, he removed his boots, socks, and clothing, turned, and pulled the bedspread and sheet on the bed down and laid down, pulling the sheet and bed spread up to his chest. *Seemed to be high livin' for a kid from Missouri*, he thought. Laying there, his hands were feeling the material that the bed spread was made of. It was a cotton-like material and had little tufts of cotton-like balls all over it. He rubbed it with his hand and liked the feel of it.

But then his mind came to the present when Kathryn moved a little. He could tell that she was stretching because he felt her arms, shaking a bit, move upwards over her head and her back and legs stiffen.

Very softly she said, "I need to go pee Ponder. I'll be right back."

Back she came, slid back under the blanket, and once more moved as close as humanly possible up against his back. Her arm came over his side and her hand was flat against his chest. It was very early morning and the drops of dew could be heard falling through the leaves of the bush they had slept under. Never before in Ponder's entire life had he experienced something as totally comforting as laying here with this woman, now named Kathryn, pulled up against him.

Quietly, Ponder said to her, "Kathryn, you have no idea who I even am."
Kathryn responded just as quietly with, "Ponder, I think that I really do!"
Another hour passed before it was totally daylight.

"Kathryn," Ponder said, "We need to get up, have some coffee and some of that dried meat, and head out."

"What do you want me to do Ponder?" said Kathryn. "I can get some water and start our coffee, if you will get a fire started."

Ponder replied, "I'll build you a little fire."

He then pulled the blanket from him but not Kathryn, got to his feet with Kathryn right behind him, reached for his clothes, and quickly got dressed. Then he walked to where the fire was the day before and, down on one knee, began to gather small pieces of wood and some dry grasses. He made a pile, took the flint and knife from his pocket, and quickly sparked a small smoky fire that would grow quickly to the point that some larger wood pieces could be added. He was mindful to keep his back to Kathryn to allow her the opportunity for a bit of privacy to dress. It was only a minute before she was squatted beside him poking in the new built fire with a small twig. Ponder glanced at Kathryn who wearing a happy smile.

She said, "Good morning Ponder."

"Good morning to you too, Kathryn," said Ponder. "I will break some coffee beans so you can make that coffee."

As he went to the saddlebag lying in the rocks to get a handful of coffee beans, Kathryn retrieved the small coffee pot, carried it to the creek and, taking up some water, swished the water around in the pot to remove anything loose in it.

"How much water do we need Ponder?" asked Kathryn, "Would about half the pot be enough?"

"Just a little more than that," Ponder replied.

Using his kerchief, a flat rock, and the butt of his Navy Colt as a hammer, Ponder broke the beans into tiny pieces. He picked up the four corners of the kerchief, allowing the crushed coffee to meander to the center of the kerchief, stood up and carried it to Kathryn who was back at the small fire. Looking at Kathryn, she turned her head towards him for some direction and their eyes met. In Ponder's mind, this was how it should be between a man and a woman. The look in her eyes was not of someone he had just met, but of someone that he had known forever. At that moment, he felt closer to Kathryn than he had ever figured he would. All of this had happened so fast that Ponder found it hard to understand why he suddenly had felt closeness to this woman Kathryn.

While the coffee was cooking on the fire, Ponder picked up the saddle blanket from the ground and shook everything from it that he could. Walking to Lilly, who was grazing nearby, he walked with the blanket to her while she stood and watched him come toward her. Ponder carefully brushed Lilly's back off with his hand, where the blanket would contact her body. He then walked around Lilly inspecting her legs and feet. Then, coming to the other side of her, stroked her head, scratched the ridge of her nose, and tousled her mane, telling her the entire time what a good girl she was. When he turned, he met Kathryn who had the blanket they slept under. It had been shaken out, doubled, and rolled as she had seen it on Ponders rig. Ponder took the blanket from her and laid it gently across the hind quarter of Lilly. Lilly whinnied a bit and lifted one back leg from the ground, shifting her weight. Then to the saddle, which Ponder turned over and checked to ensure that no burrs or objects were fastened to the skirt of the saddle. Then picking the saddle up, he gingerly tossed it aboard Lilly and reached for the girth belt to make the saddle fast. All that was left was the bridle, which Ponder retrieved and gently placed on Lilly's head.

Then, meeting Kathryn back at the rocks they had sat on the day before, he handed her a few little pieces of the dried meat as she handed him the cup of coffee that they would have to share. At first they sat in silence.

"I wish I had some sugar for your coffee Kathryn," said Ponder.

After a while, Kathryn said, "The coffee is great, Ponder. Sometimes we wish for things that cannot make anything taste better, we only imagine it will. You are a hundred times the man that Albert was. No, you are thousands times more than Albert was. Had I laid down with him before marriage as I did you, he would have had me. You are a man, a good man, and probably the best I will ever meet."

Ponder looked at Kathryn, but did not reply.

With the coffee pot rinsed out and stored in the saddle bag, Ponder mounted Lilly, reached out with his hand, and helped Kathryn aboard behind him. Once seated, Kathryn placed her arms around Ponder and held him tightly as they rode off to the Northeast.

Chapter 13

⊷⇒ ⇐⊷

Supper with Vermin

Ponder enjoyed a restful sleep for a few hours on the hotel bed. He slowly came awake realizing that he was hungry. Getting up and stretching, with his hands washing any sleep from his eyes, Ponder dressed. He looked at himself in a mirror that was mounted on the wall in his room, returned to the wash basin, and wet his hair enough that it lay flat on his head. He put on his little jacket and hat and retrieved the Navy Colt which he stuck in his waistband. Going to the corner where the Henry stood, he picked it up and slid it beneath the bed. He looked at himself in the mirror again, unlocked the door, and walked out. Then he closed the door, once again locking it, and placing the key in his jacket pocket. Then he went down the hall and stairs to the hotel lobby and onto the walk outside. Fixing his hat, Ponder stepped from the walk onto the dirt street and across it to the Saloon.

Once inside, through the smoke, he saw the area they must have considered the restaurant part of the saloon. Back in the corner and to the right was an area with square table, rather than the round tables in the saloon area. There were a few people, all men, sitting in the square table area. Some were eating and some were seemingly talking and waiting for the woman. She had seen setting something on a table and returned through a door to what must be the kitchen. Ponder walked to the corner of the eating area and chose an un occupied table, taking a chair facing the saloon door, and sat down. He removed his hat and set it in the chair to his right.

In just a few minutes, the lady he had seen flitting back and forth to the kitchen was standing at the table in front of him. She was a young girl with rosy cheeks and a bead of sweat coming from her hairline, down the side of her face. She had an apron on that had blue and white checks. She had a nice demeanor.

"Sir," she said, "What would you like to have to eat?"

Ponder replied, "Would you mind telling me my choices?"

With her right index finger on her right cheek and looking to the side she said, "Well, we have beef steak, fried potatoes with onion. We have stew, which is cut up steak with carrots, potatoes, and onion. We have something like chicken with dumplings and we can fix eggs, bacon, and biscuits. Oh! And we have a pie tonight. It's peach pie." Leaning forward she said, "The pie is good, I had some of it." Ponder inquired if they had any hot bread, which brought the answer, "We have some corn bread!"

Ponder said that he would like some of the stew, a few pieces of corn bread, and a large slice of that peach pie with a cup of coffee.

"Coming right up," the girl said and away through the door she went.

Through the saloon door, a man came. He was dressed like a "city" person. Slightly overweight and wearing a derby of sorts. Ruddy type complexion, he looked like a Yankee. The man looked around for a short while and then looked back to the corner where Ponder sat. He came over. Walking up to the other side of Ponder's table, the man asked if he might join him.

"That will be fine," replied Ponder.

No effort was made by the man to introduce himself. He pulled the opposing chair from the table and sat down. He also did not remove his hat. The girl working there showed up from the kitchen, delivering a plate of food to a man sitting a few tables away, and Ponder's new guest, seeing her, yelled a profanity at her and told her to get her ass over here. Ponder was taken aback with his guest's manner. The guest harshly told the girl that he wanted a steak rare, some potatoes, and a mug of beer from the bar. He also told her that if she didn't have his food out quickly that she would be sorry.

The young girl was shaken by this. She said, "I'll try mister."

To which he replied, "You little bitch, you better do more than try." As she walked away the man said, "You have to keep these people in line."

Ponder replied, "Is that right?" in a questioning tone.

"I haven't seen you around here, who are you?" the man said.

"Just a traveler," answered Ponder. "Out this way to see if I can find a pile of rocks to buy and live on."

The man sat and looked at Ponder for about thirty seconds and said, "I don't see how you might buy anything, especially a piece of land. God, you don't look like you can even have enough to eat in this joint, much less buy a piece of property."

Ponder replied, "Sometimes you just never know, do you?"

With this, the man pardoned himself and said that he needed to see a guy across the street before he left for the day. He pushed his chair out , headed to the front door, and left. By now, Ponder wished that he had told the man that he wished to eat alone.

Watching the front door, Ponder saw one man walk in and go to the end of the saloon bar where he stood with a foot on the bar rail. Moments later, Ponder's favorite guest came back through the door, headed to the table where Ponder sat, and resumed his seat across from Ponder. In a few minutes, two more men came through the saloon door and walked to the restaurant area, taking a seat in the other corner of the eating area. Both were facing him and his guest. Just about that time, the little rosy-cheeked girl came to the table carrying Ponder's food order. She sat it down and seemed nervous to be within reach of the guest.

Ponder broke off a piece of the corn bread and dove it into the stew. With a spoon, he lifted the piece of cornbread, now covered in stew, and placed it in his mouth. Hungry or not, this stew was good. He continued to eat the food he ordered, not paying a lot of attention to the obnoxious guest at the table.

If this stew tastes this good, thought Ponder, *I bet that peach pie is every bit as good as that girl said.*

Eventually, the guest said that he had heard of a piece of property just North of Comfort that was up for sale by some German, "Maybe a section or so I heard."

Ponder replied, "That sounds pretty good. Anybody know what he is asking for it?"

"You saying you'd have the money to possibly buy it?" said the guest.

"Nope," said Ponder, "You're asking the questions, I'm just trying to eat and be congenial."

Ponder feared that he knew where all this was going. He was hoping to get some of the peach pie eaten before it did.

"With expectations such as you have, finding and buying a piece of land and all, I figure you got the money to accomplish your task," said the guest at the table.

Ponder continued to eat and the girl was right, the peach pie was really good. He finished the last bite of his pie and then, with the side of the fork, gathered up the little pie stuff that was left on the plate it was served on. With that, Ponder laid his fork next to the plate the pie had been served on and placed his hands on the table edge.

Still looking at his plate, Ponder said quietly, "I figure I knew where this was going when you left and gathered three no goods like yourself so you might accomplish the task of taking my money. I have enough money to pay for this meal, pay for my hotel room, and to bail Lilly out of the livery in the morning. I also have enough money to replace the paper cartridges in my Colt that I am going to use to kill you and your three friends. So, how bad do you want my money?"

"Ain't talking about no dinner money boy. I'm talking about cattle money. I know who you are, you're one of them took them Longhorn to Sedalia." Turning his head, the guest surveyed his cohorts, nodded at them, and then said, "Got a pistol under this table. If you don't pull that money and put it on the table, I'm going to gut shoot you."

With that, Ponder quickly grabbed his edge of the table, throwing it upwards which made the guest's side of the table go down, causing the gun being held by the guest to discharge in the floor between his own legs. Even before the round from the guest's gun hit the floor, Ponder had his Navy out with his arm holding it extended across the wrecked table.

"Holler at that girl, asshole," said Ponder. "You are going to pay her before you leave this world. It took some coaxing before the guest could muster up the words to summon the young girl who had taken his order, but finally he succeeded."

Frightfully and hesitantly, the red-cheeked girl slowly made her way to the table where Ponder held the man pinned with the muzzle of his .36.

"How much does this man owe you young lady?" Ponder asked the girl, without taking his eyes from the guest.

"That would be two dollars and ten cents," said the girl.

"Pay the lady," said Ponder.

The guest was frightened and shaking, but fished a roll of money from an inside vest pocket.

"How much you got there?" Ponder asked the guest.

"I don't know, maybe three hundred dollars," said the guest.

"Give it to the girl, it will be a nice tip and honestly you ain't gonna need it."

The guest shoved the money towards the girl and Ponder told her to take it. He also told her to go to the kitchen. Ponder looked up quickly to check the status of the guest's three friends. They were seemingly frozen in time, hands part way to their pistols. The saloon was understandably quiet.

"There is no time like the present," Ponder said as he dropped the hammer and fired a .36 caliber ball into the guest's forehead, then turned, firing and hitting the two men at the table to his right square in the chest.

Then a short turn to his left lined him up with the third man who had been standing at the bar, near the door. The third man had not even cleared his holster with his handgun by this time. He looked as if he was just going to quit what he intended to do. He let his revolver fall on back into the holster, raised his hand up from his belt, and it was just about then that Ponder fired his fourth round, the ball hitting man number three about an inch lower than the top button on his shirt. The noise was still echoing when man number three fell to the saloon floor. Glancing back at the two that had been at the table, he noted that one of them had rolled a bit on his side and was trying his best to work his revolver.

Ponder walked closer to the guy that was still moving, pointed his Navy colt at the man's head and said, "This is a poor line of work you have chosen cause you ain't very good at it," and fired his fifth round, hitting the man just behind his right ear.

There was no movement in the saloon. No talk, no glasses tinkling, no sound at all. Ponder stuck the Navy back in his belt, walked to the kitchen, and placed three dollars on a shelf for his meal.

Knowing fully that some police officer would invariably show up soon, Ponder whisked out the saloon door, crossed the street to the Gist Hotel, and went up to his room. He unlocked the door and entered, gathered his Henry from beneath the bed, his extra shirt, and razor, and was gone from the Gist. A few doors down, where the livery was, he went to the stall where Lilly was. He stood the Henry in the corner with his spare shirt atop the barrel. He then saddled Lilly ready for travel. Then stuck the spare shirt and razor in his saddle bag and the Henry back to the scabbard. The light of a kerosene lamp suddenly appeared carried by Hickham, the liverier.

Ponder asked Mr. Hickham what he owed him and in a minute the Liverier said, "I think that a couple of dollars would do it young man."

Ponder handed him what he thought was four dollars, said "thank you", mounted Lilly, and headed out of Austin.

Ponder thought better about going directly back to his camp from the night before and instead decided to strike a trail South and spend a day or so before returning to the camp just west of Austin to retrieve the empty peach can hidden under the rock.

Late the next morning, he was at the Guadalupe River southwest of Austin. It had been a long night. He stopped for a while, rested Lilly, laid in some soft grasses, and slept for a short while. He made no coffee when he woke up and, since all of his provisions were depleted except for a sack of dried beans, he ate nothing. He had plenty to eat the night before in Austin. That was a town that he probably needed to stay clear of for a while after the dealings in the saloon. The part of it he had seen he cared not to see again anyway. Ponder decided to clean himself and his clothes in the river and then take a nap while his clothes dried. He could stay here this night and head back to west of Austin tomorrow to collect his money from beneath the big flat rock.

Chapter 14

‑‑■● ●■‑‑

Peaches in a Can

Lilly carried both Ponder and Kathryn easily. They were moving at a leisurely pace. Lilly would bob her head now and then and snort and that, plus the sound of her hooves on the ground, was about the only sound about.

For about a half hour there was silence and then Kathryn said, "What do you have ahead of you Ponder?"

"Looks like trees, rocks, and hills to me Kathryn," he responded.

"That's not what I mean Ponder. I mean are you headed someplace in particular?"

"Kathryn," Ponder said, "We are headed to a place close to Austin to pick up a can of peaches. We are headed West from there, but I can't tell you where exactly."

"We're going to Austin to *buy* a can of peaches Ponder?"

"Well," said Ponder, "Not exactly. I had my fill of Austin the other night and I am thinking that I need to stay out of Austin, especially right now, but we will be just west of Austin before turning West."

"Ponder," said Kathryn, "Are you going to let me go with you wherever it is that you are going?"

Ponder was silent for quite a way. He could sense that Kathryn was tense from the way her hands clung to the sides of his body as they rode. Actually, he did not know how to answer her. His intention was to find a piece of land and live on it. He had never known women, or even a woman. He had certainly never lay naked with a woman under a blanket that was as naked as he was.

He never knew how soft a woman was, how good it felt for one to lay against you, or kiss you on your forehead. A woman had never been in his plan as he had never expected more than to pass one on a street or bump into one in a shop in some little town. The one on the back of Lilly had a serious problem with a man, her husband, and might be a warning to him to get help. Ponder did not want to assume something was there that was never to be.

He knew nothing of women, including the one sitting behind him with her arms tight to his waist. There was a thing he had heard long ago about counting chickens before they hatch and he feared that might be the case. He was simply looking for some land to settle on. But for what? If he found a place and worked it somehow to make a living from it, for what would he do that? Just to live there, work on the place, and one day die, presuming the Comanches didn't get him first.

Perhaps when he reached his old camp west of Austin where his "poke" was rolled in an empty peach can he might learn more. There was no way that he could retrieve that can without Kathryn knowing exactly what the can held. Would he be able to judge by the look in her eyes or her demeanor when she saw the money? Ponder liked this woman. If she had really done what she professed, she was a tough person and for that he admired her. Working out a relationship with her would fill the bill of life he had in mind, for some day. But that might not even be close to what the woman now called Kathryn was looking for.

Finally, Ponder replied to Kathryn's question, "Kathryn, I think that it is only you that will be able to answer the question you asked me. When we get those peaches," Ponder said, "I will explain some things and we can go from there. Might be that what I have in my mind is something you would rather not partake of and could be that I would not want you to."

Kathryn seemed to relax a bit as her hands flattened a bit on his sides. She also had the side of her head against his back.

Probably about six hours had passed and the only time that they had stopped was when Kathryn asked if she could use the privy. Ponder exclaimed that Lilly probably would like to rest for a while and that the privy idea might suit him as well. Ponder helped Kathryn slide from the back of Lilly and then dismounted himself. Kathryn patted Ponder on his leg before he dismounted and she walked off through the nearby brush. Ponder walked the opposite direction and relieved himself as well. He was first to return to where Lilly stood.

He had removed his hat and poured a bit of water from his canteen in it and was letting Lilly have a drink from it. Lilly's big brown eyes signaled that Kathryn was returning.

Ponder held the canteen out for Kathryn to rinse her hands with some water and handed her a kerchief from his saddlebag to dry her hands and wipe her face if she wished. He did the same except for not wiping his face. She was surely a graceful creature. When she walked, the hair at her temples sort of blew back and bounced a bit with her step. Ponder stated that a ways ahead, there was a small creek that they would stop at and let Lilly rest a bit more, plus rest their rears a while. He also said that they were probably only an hour, not more than two hours, from where they were headed. Back on to Lilly's back and again they headed for the peaches.

Not more than three miles farther they reached the creek that Ponder had remembered crossing two nights ago. Again they stopped, dismounted, and Ponder removed Lilly's bridle and hung it on the saddle horn. Lilly wandered a few feet to a big patch of grass and idly ate. Kathryn took the canteen, poured the water from it, and, at the creek, stooped and refilled it with fresh water. Taking it to Ponder she held it forward that he might take it and get a drink from it.

Ponder said, "I think the lady goes first, doesn't she?"

Kathryn blushed and smiled saying, "Thank you sir."

The canteen was put to her lips and she drank with her eyes on Ponder the entire length of time it took for the drink of water. She passed the canteen to Ponder.

Taking it, he said, "Thank you Ma'am."

The canteen was refilled then and both laid down on the big patch of grass that was being consumed in snitch-like bites by Lilly. It was quiet, there was no conversation. After a while, Ponder told Kathryn that the need get Lilly ready and finish their trip. After bridling Lilly and Ponder mounting her and helping Kathryn aboard, they were again on the way to the big rocky hill that lied just west of Austin, Texas. As Ponder had said, it took about one and a half hours to reach his camp from two nights before and the big flat rock lying by the big cedar tree. But it was a guess because Ponder never owned a watch.

Down through a ravine and then up the hill to the camp, Lilly carried Ponder and Kathryn. Ponder was watchful that no other people were around. As traveled as the area was with folks headed to Austin, it was likely that someone could easily just show up near them. Reaching the area that was the camp before, Ponder once again helped Kathryn from the back of Lilly and stepped out of the saddle and onto the ground with a sweeping eye.

"Kathryn," Ponder said, "Would you mind gathering some small wood, enough for fire enough to make a pot of coffee."

"I would be glad to," said Kathryn and she started canvassing the area for the wood needed for a fire. Meanwhile Ponder, using his boot, worked at pushing the small circle of rocks to build a fire in back together from when he had separated the when leaving this camp before. Still he was moving around the rock circle, using that time to view the area looking for people about.

Some beans and little coffee pot were retrieved from the saddlebag and again crushed in Ponder's kerchief against a rock. They were put in the little coffee pot and, with some water added from the canteen, were waiting for fire to turn them into coffee. Kathryn soon had some wood pieces gathered and, with some dead grasses to help, Ponder stooped and quickly made a spark to ignite the light, dry matter and soon got a small fire going on which the coffee pot was placed. From the look on Kathryn's face, Ponder knew that she had no idea of what this was all about. It had passed being a mystery to her. Soon, a bit of steam escaped the little coffee pot and the smell of the coffee erupted at the camp.

Ponder once more went to his saddlebag and gathered the one cup he had and some of the dried meat they had prepared and saved for later. He also retrieved the Henry from the scabbard on his saddle and, walking back over the camp area, leaned it against the remains of a long dead cedar.

"Kathryn," said Ponder, "Come sit down and let me pour us a drink of coffee." Kathryn had not said much at all since getting off Lilly when they arrived at this camp. "All we have to eat is some of our dried meat. I'll do better tomorrow."

Kathryn walked over and sat in the grass next to Ponder. "I'm grateful to have what we have Ponder. Right now that word 'tomorrow' makes me feel better. I was afraid that from here you were going to get sick of me, leaving me near enough to a town that I would have a place to seek a life to live," said Kathryn.

"If that was your wish Kathryn, you are free to make that choice. But honestly, that is not what I had in mind. I know all this seems strange and mysterious, but I think that soon you will have some understanding of what my plan is," Ponder said. "After I explain my intent, you might decide to walk down the hill into Austin. Then again, you might not."

Sitting there, each taking an occasional sip of the coffee, Ponder, in a summary as short as possible, covered his life's experience including his childhood, the war, the cattle drive, Walt, the peach can under the rock, the day in Austin, and all else, right up to the point in time they were at right at this very moment. It truly was a short summary and he hoped that Kathryn would understand such a long tale told so quickly. They were sharing the one tin cup and as Kathryn passed the cup back to Ponder.

She said, "Are you saying that if I wish to go with you I may?" She stood and faced Ponder. "Ponder," spoke Kathryn very seriously, "I've not known many men. I married the first one that paid me a mind and it was a mistake. In just these few hours, I have learned the difference in what a real man is instead of just a guy dressed as one. If you wish for me to go, for god's sake, tell me now. Otherwise, when we get back on Lilly you will have me forever because I am not going anywhere. And I don't give a damn about the can of peaches."

"Kathryn," inquired Ponder, "Do you know what Utopia is?"

"Isn't that supposed to be the perfect place and everyone has been looking for it since the beginning of time?" asked Kathryn, having the cup handed back to her by Ponder.

"I think that is a fair description of what Utopia was described to me once. Kathryn, I want you to understand *fully* that I don't think that is where we are headed. That would not be a good place to wind up. But I don't know if where we will end up will be that place."

Ponder stood and glanced around fully once more and walked the few steps to the big, flat rock. Grasping it by the front edge, he lifted it and let it lay back against the cedar tree as he had done before. In the crevice he had made by moving the dirt and rocks with his boot was the can for the peaches he had eaten that had been replaced by four thousand, seven hundred, and forty-something dollars. As he stood erect with the can in hand, he glanced once more at his surroundings and still saw no one in sight. He held the can out towards Kathryn. She took the several steps to where he stood and took the can from Ponders hand. He stepped from there to behind the big flat rock and pushed it back to its original resting place.

Walking the few steps to where she stood looking at the huge roll of money rolled into the empty peach can, Ponder said, "That is mine and Walt's share of the cattle money I told you about Kathryn."

Kathryn walked to Lilly and placed the can in Pander's saddle bag then went back to Ponder. Ponder offered Kathryn a piece of the dried meat that he had taken earlier from the same saddle bag, took the tin cup, and put the remnants of the coffee from the little pot, that was still by the small fire, into it.

"Let's sit a minute and I will tell you what my intentions are Kathryn."

She wasn't frowning nor was she smiling, but rather had a shocked look on her face. They both sat.

"West of here is a trading post at a place they call Llano. It's just a small settlement I've been told, that was a while back," said Ponder. "It is a one or two day ride from where we sit. We are going to head that direction and once we get there I'm going to ask around to see if there is land near there to be purchased. If perchance there is such a thing and it looks like a piece of property that I could hammer out a living of sorts on, I'm going to try to buy it. If there is nothing there that can be bought or made a living on we will head either further West or South, depending on what we might hear people say. When we get to the Llano area, we very well may hide the money again, as I have done here. If we find a piece of property, we will find a spot on it where a person can live safely and comfortably. But we are not going to let people see this money. That could bring trouble."

Chapter 15

⊶⟫ ⟪⊶

Headed to Llano

Not wanting to waste the water from the canteen, the grounds in it were dumped as best as Kathryn could. With it and the one tin cup packed in a saddle bag, they mounted Lilly and moved away to the West. The sun was still a fair piece above the horizon, so they had time to make some miles before stopping again for the night. Kathryn seemed to be relaxed but was holding Ponder a bit more tightly than before he felt. A little way out, Ponder asked Kathryn if she was alright.

"Ponder," she replied, "I quite possibly have never been as alright as I am at this very moment." Her head turned sideways and was once again her body was buried as close as possible as she could get it into his back.

"I am hoping that we can find a creek or something by nightfall," said Ponder. "Lilly is going to need a good drink of water soon. Pickings for supper are going to be pretty slim, we still have some dried meat but not much."

As luck would have it, in an hour or so, with the sun just slightly above the horizon, their trail crossed a small creek that had a small amount of water moving down it. About twenty feet from the creek was a huge live oak tree. It was one of those that had limbs reaching out that touched the ground and rose again. Kathryn thought the limbs looked like giant serpents that she had read about in the school she had attended as a child. Out near the end of the longest limb, was a stand of brush and that is where they decided to rest for the night.

Checking his saddle bag, which by now had been removed from Lilly when he unfastened the saddle and lifted it from Lilly's back, there were just enough coffee beans left for coffee to be made in his little one-man pot. Kathryn, anticipating that Ponder would want to make coffee for the evening, had already started picking up small dead fall from the area beneath the oak.

Someone had camped here before because there were remnants of a fire from long ago that had been build in a small circle of rock that were still in place. After gathering the small amount of wood and tinder need for the fire, Kathryn walked to Ponder and asked for the fire flint and his knife, which he readily handed her. Kathryn had never in her life started a fire as Ponder did. She wanted to not only prove to herself that she could do it, but also show Ponder her willingness to take part.

Ponder made himself busy, first by removing the bridle from Lilly and spending some time with her, rubbing her back and face, scratching under her neck, and then inspecting her feet and legs. He owed Lilly that, she had been a good horse.

He broke some beans and then took the little pot to the creek and squatted down to gather some water in it. He was careful not to take up any sediment from the creek bottom, so he just laid the pot on its side and let the water run into it. Doing this several times to rinse it, he then captured some for making the coffee. He then poured the broken coffee beans in the pot with that water. As he stood and turned in the direction of where the fire ring was, there was Kathryn sitting on her rear facing him with legs out in front of her and crossed. She was leaning back using her arms to hold her up and she had a huge grin on her face. Beside her, there was a small growing fire.

Cocking her head to one side, she asked, "How's that for a fire Ponder?"

Ponder replied that it was the fastest and best fire he had ever seen, to which Kathryn seemed to nearly glow in the declining light of the day. Standing there for an instant, Ponder felt something within him that he had never felt before. It felt good to him. He was thinking that he was glad that Kathryn had showed up and that his Colt was unloaded the first day. He also was happy that she had not decided to try her luck in Austin. If Kathryn was this delighted, she had no idea how much he was also. It was a lonely life he had led , a short one, but lonely. With the coffee made and a portion in the one cup that they had to share, Kathryn exclaimed that the coffee was possibly the best that she had ever tasted. When Ponder delivered her some of the dried meat, she even bragged about it.

Chapter 16

⊹⟾ ⟽⊹

In Questions

As Ponder was finishing the last bit of coffee, Kathryn gathered the saddle blanket, shook it out well and, looking around, picked a place to set it on the ground. It was an area with lots of grass and no rocks. Then she did the same thing with the wool blanket. She even gathered Ponder's Henry rifle and laid it along what would be the right side of the bedding. She then went to where Ponder sat and had finished off the last of the coffee. Taking the pot from beside the little fire and the cup from Ponders hand, she walked the few steps to the creek and rinsed them in the same manner that she had seen Ponder fill the pot.

Ponder retrieved the extra kerchief from the saddlebag and untied the one from his neck. He walked to the creek and, stooping again, wet and rinsed both of them. He then turned and carried them to where Kathryn was, on the grassy patch where the pallet to sleep on had been made. He held out to her the wet kerchief that had come from the saddlebag. But before taking it from him, she shed her clothes to the ground. She bent and picked them up, rolled them into a tube and laid it at the head of the pallet on the right side of the soon to be bed.

"That can be your pillow," Kathryn said, as she took the wet kerchief from Ponders hand and began wiping her body down.

Ponder was at a total loss. He had just about lost count of the times he had seen this woman naked. He knew not whether she was inviting him or testing him. It was difficult, but he decided to take what she was doing as just

61

a matter of trust and make nothing of it. Ponder, still a bit bashful, once again turned from Kathryn and removed his boots and his clothing. He then remembered that the peach can was still in the saddle bag and, trying to not put on much of a show, retrieved the can full of money from the saddlebag and stuck it in the fork of three limbs of a bush nearby. Then he took the few steps back to the pallet. In looking at the pillow of sorts that Kathryn had made for him from her clothing, he did the same with his and, helping her rise up a bit, placed it beneath her head. He then laid down and pulled the blanket part way over the two of them. Kathryn, just as the night before, lay there gazing at the stars in the Texas sky and once again Ponder could see the reflection of those stars in her eyes.

"Ponder," Kathryn said in a questioning tone. "Are you a gambler?"

"I guess I am," Ponder said, after a minute or so. "Driving those cattle to Missouri was a gamble."

"Not like that Ponder," said Kathryn. "I mean, do you play cards for money or other games like that?"

"Well," replied Ponder, "I've never had anything to gamble with, nor desired to sit with the people that I saw gambling. Not saying I never would Kathryn, but I never have and may never want to."

About then, Lilly, munching on grasses close to them, snorted and Ponder saw her move in the direction from which they came. Ponder heard the movement of rocks and then a light clacking noise. He had instantly touched Kathryn's side with his left hand and laid his hand across the wrist of his Henry when Lilly made her noise, but Ponder realized quickly that they were in no danger. They were hearing a couple of Armadillos turning manageable sized rocks over looking for bugs or some other food. He quietly told Kathryn what they were hearing and she laughed, grabbing Ponders left hand with her right hand.

"If I was yours, Ponder, and if you gambled and lost, would you try to settle your debt with what you can't, but I can, do?" asked Kathryn.

A minute or two passed, because Ponder wanted to be careful with his answer. "Kathryn," said Ponder softly, "You need to try to forget that part of your life. It happened and I doubt the memory of it will ever leave you. Your sorry husband deserved what you gave him and more. But realize Kathryn that you are not 'mine'. Right now, we are just two folks out here trying to get by with what we have to work with," said Ponder. "I have not one time even thought about having a wife, partner, or such, Kathryn. I have never had anything to offer anyone that I might even consider marrying. I have been pretty busy just trying to keep myself going most of my life."

"But you do have something to offer Ponder," replied Kathryn.

"Now that I have a peach can full of money I do I guess Kathryn. But until now, I have lived from the fat of the land and I'm telling you that in these times that land isn't very fat."

"No," Kathryn said, "The money you have right now is not the best thing you have to offer Ponder. Not that the money won't make life more comfortable maybe, but you are *you* without or with the money. I so wish that somehow it had been you that came along instead of Albert. I had something to offer him that I no longer have. And even with him gone I will never have it to offer again."

Ponder, although not wise of the world, knew what Kathryn was trying to tell him. He was sad for her thoughts because he knew that she *would* be judged for that by whoever might consider making a life with her.

"But no Kathryn," proclaimed Ponder, "I would never have used you to pay off a debt. I would hope that before I even proposed such a thing to you that lightning would strike me dead."

"I exposed myself to you when we first met so that you would not think that I was meek. I laid naked with you because I did not have to be meek and had run into the most decent human being that I think ever walked. I am as comfortable around you as I am with the clothes your head is on right now," said Kathryn.

"When I kiddingly called you 'Purty'," said Ponder, "I should have called you 'beautiful' Kathryn. I know the difference. I know what I look like because I see my face in the water when I am shaving sometimes and I ain't 'Purty'. With that I have little to offer, Kathryn. We need to get some rest now because we need to make Llano tomorrow. We are out of any necessities."

"That's fine," said Kathryn. "But we need to talk some more tomorrow about this."

Just before Ponder closed his eyes, he felt the softness of Kathryn's body close the distance between them and she placed her left arm across his chest.

Chapter 17

⟨⟩

On to Llano

Kathryn was up with the morning and went about gathering enough material to build another small fire to make the last of their coffee. She had gently removed the pillow made from her clothing from beneath Ponder's head. She had a fire going even before he rose, stretched, and dressed. Walking to Lilly, he rubbed her head and asked her if she was ready for another day. He picked the Henry up and stood it against a tree then shook the blankets out and placed the saddle blanket on Lilly's back for when he put the saddle on later. He then rolled the wool blanket and laid it on a rock a few feet away. Reaching in saddle bag for the remaining coffee, he discovered that it was gone because Kathryn already had it in the kerchief and was grinding the coffee beans using two stones.

With the coffee done, they again sat on the rocks and shared the cup. They also finished off the dried meat they had. There was not a lot of conversation this morning. Pondering was considering what he might find out about some land that possibly might be for sale. Kathryn was wondering the same thing, but also how she might convey her feelings about Ponder to him. So far as Kathryn was concerned, she *was* his. She heard Ponder say the night before that she was not, but Ponder was wrong. She would never be able to look at another man without comparing him to Ponder.

With breakfast done, Ponder saddled Lilly and placed the bridle on her head. Picking his Henry up from where it leaned on the tree, he placed it in the scabbard on Lilly. Kathryn had kicked dirt on the remaining campfire and had already washed the cup and coffee pot and checked the canteen to see if it was full.

It wasn't but a couple of hours before they met the Llano River in their path. The whole trip had been made with Kathryn having her hands around Ponder's waist, more or less resting them on his legs. The river had a bank and a bed that was entirely white limestone. The river water itself seemed to have a turquoise color to it and the water, though the banks were far from full, was running swiftly. The bank of the river was easy to follow. It looked like seasonal high water had pretty well kept the growth of bushes down just along the banks. Both Ponder and Kathryn thought the sight was pleasant. Movement in the tops of a grove of oaks ahead was seen by Ponder. He knew that what he was seeing was squirrels.

It was near noon, the sun was nearly straight atop them. They rode just past the grove of oaks and stopped. It was a very flat area within ten or so feet of the river. Ponder proclaimed to Kathryn that with a bit of luck that he was going to bark a few squirrels so that they could have some lunch. In anticipation of that, Kathryn, with the help of Ponder, slid from Lilly's backside. Ponder slipped off as well, pulling his Henry from its scabbard as he stepped down.

"Kathryn," said Ponder. "Give me a minute and if I am lucky with this I'd like for you to build us a fire."

Within moments, there were shots from the Henry at the tree just under where a squirrel was, he had four squirrels on the ground. Quickly Ponder removed the entrails and skinned the squirrels and it was Kathryn's turn with Ponder's knife and, retrieving the flint from the saddle bag, she had wood gathered and a small fire built so fast it shocked Ponder. Retrieving the small piece of wire from his saddlebag that he had used to dry the venison a few days before, he strung the squirrel carcasses and had the wire suspended on two sticks no more than six to eight inches above the fire. Remembering his small sack of salt, he retrieved it and sprinkled a bit on the squirrels being cooked.

Ponder looked up at Kathryn, "I guess that we aren't going to starve after all."

"I don't figure I ever will Ponder, as long as I have you," Kathryn replied, "And I figure that to be a long, long time, because like it or not Ponder, I *am* yours."

"Kathryn, I won't say that I don't have feelings for you even though we just met," said Ponder in a low voice. "But I think that you are so fearful after what you have been through, that you are just desperate to find someone that won't hurt you."

In about an hour, the four squirrels were a golden brown. Ponder retrieved the wire they were strung on and hung the wire over a small tree limb.

"We'll let these cool for just a minute Kathryn and I'll get one off the wire for you."

They cooled just a bit and Ponder pulled one of them off the wire and handed it to Kathryn and then one for him. They made busy pulling the cooked meat from the squirrels and both remarked how good it tasted. Lilly had gone to the river's edge and spent some time taking water. She drifted around the area, having bites of grass, shaking her head and swishing her tail.

Soon, the meal was finished and the wire rolled back into a circle for storage in the saddle bag. They washed their hands in the Llano River. Ponder shoved the Henry back into the scabbard, they shared a cup of water from the Llano, mounted Lilly, and plodded off up river towards the site of Llano.

Chapter 18

꙳⚬꙳

The Trading Post

Sometime about mid afternoon, they saw a few buildings ahead that appeared to be along the bank of the river. Once reaching the settlement, they saw a trading post and a few low buildings scattered about the area. They rode in and tied Lilly to a post just outside the trading post. Ponder again helped Kathryn get down from where she sat behind him on Lilly and the swung himself down from Lilly's back. Sliding the Henry from its scabbard and holding it in his left hand, he took Kathryn with his right hand and walked toward the door of the trading post.

Ponder had about forty dollars of loose money stuck in his boot, just in case there were some supplies available they might gather for the next few days. The trading post was a building of not much height, constructed of logs, and had a room off to one side that appeared to be made of adobe. Ponder figured the adobe room must be the living quarters of the proprietor.

Walking through the door from the sunlight, there was smells of leather, rope, and many that could not be identified just yet. It had a dirt floor and the walls were plastered with every type of pan, tool, or pot imaginable. Setting on the floor was a head of cheese and that was partnered with a can of crackers. They could see sacks of salt, pepper, beans, and even a large drum of sugar. On one wall were cans of lard, peaches, beans and bottles of whiskey. The place was filled to the brim.

From behind a pile of merchandise walked a little fat man who walked up to them, extended his hand to Ponder, nodded his head to Kathryn, and introduced himself as Vernon Knott. Then Vernon asked what he could do for them. He also asked if they were new to the area. Ponder told Mr. Knott that they had just ridden in and would need some supplies. Ponder told Mr. Knott that they liked the way the county looked and were wondering perhaps if there might be a place up for sale round about. Ponder also asked Mr. Knott if there was a man of God about. With this, Kathryn turned her head and looked at Ponder.

"Mr. Ponder, is that what it was?" said Mr. Knott.

Ponder said, "It's just Ponder."

"Well Ponder, I am fairly certain that I can fill your bill for some supplies. However, I have to tell you that we got no credit."

"Wasn't looking for any," replied Ponder.

"And secondly, there are a couple of places south of here towards Fredericksburg that is for sale. Both places would be fine to raise goats or sheep, but there's not enough grass for cattle through the year, just rocky land mostly. As for the man of God, there is a reverend that passes through here about three or four times a week. He lives in a settlement just west of here. Would you be needing him for something?"

"Mr. Knott," said Ponder, "I have a small amount of cash and will need not ask for credit. I would like to know how to contact the owners of the property you mentioned and be directed to the places of interest to us. About the reverend, I might be needing him after a few days."

"Somebody with you dying?" asked Mr. Knott.

"No sir, I would just like to ask him a question. We would like to camp around here until we find out if the places you know about are truly available, if that would suit the community."

"Ponder," said Mr. Knott, "I have a little building, sort of a house, just across the street that kind of serves as the local hotel for our community of Llano. The rate is fifty cents a day. There is a German woman just down the street that will cook for you for fifty cents a day and that's for you both. She's a pretty good cook, she only speaks German but she's a clean person. Right behind this store is a stable where you might keep your horse. I have a Mexican boy that will bring feed in for him."

"It's a her," said Ponder.

"Anyway," said Knott, "Thirty cents a day keeps your horse."

Ponder looked at Kathryn and she had a look of delight about her.

70

"Plus," Knott said, "When the Minister comes through, if you ain't gone looking, I'll point him your way."

"Reckon we can go look at the little house Mr. Knott?" inquired Ponder.

"You betcha," said Knott. "It's open."

Knott turned and walked back into the trading post. Ponder and Kathryn turned the other direction and walked across to the little house. The house had a small porch with a roof over it held up by two wooded beams. On the porch was a small stack of wood cut for firewood. The house itself was a structure covered by planks of sawed wood. That meant that there was a sawmill somewhere nearby. The inside walls were the other side of the wood seen on the outside of the house. There were two little windows on the front of the house with shutters that lifted to the inside. Walking through the door, they could see that it had one room. In one corner was a bed of good size and was made up to be slept in. Along one wall there was a rack where clothes might be hung and next to it, a mirror on the wall with two little hooks that held a couple of towels. Along the back wall was a small, simple fireplace with a bucket of kindling. There was a small table with a couple of candles on it by one of the windows and there were two wooden chairs hanging on pegs in the wall. The little house had a rough-sawed wooden floor. The only other items were a clay pot, undoubtedly for holding water, and a clay privy pot.

"Looks good to me," said Ponder.

"It's wonderful," said Kathryn.

Ponder replied that he would go make arrangements for them to have the house for a week or so and asked Kathryn if she would like to see if Mr. Knott had some clothes that she might purchase.

"That would be nice. May I do that?" Kathryn said.

"I think you should," replied Ponder, "You need more than just what you have on." Ponder stood the Henry rifle in the corner next to the front door.

So, they walked across the opening to Mr. Knott's store. Kathryn had not said much, but had a nice smile on her face. Seeing Knotts at the back, Ponder told him that the little house would serve them well and that he would like to pay up on it for a week, if that was alright.

"And," Ponder said, "If you have some paper cartridges for a .36 Navy Colt and a box of .44 Flat Henry cartridges, I'd like them as well. I also need a cup and if you have a couple of spoons or forks, I would like them and two cans of peaches also." As he had seen some on the wall.

"Kathryn," Ponder asked, "Would you like some sugar?"

To which she replied, "That would be nice, Ponder. Mr. Knott, would you happen to have a dress or some other clothes that a woman might wear?"

"That would be my wife's department," said Mr. Knott and he called her name, "Betsy, could you come out here please?"

Betsy appeared in the door from the adobe section of the building. She was wiping her hands on an apron that she wore.

"Betsy, this Kathryn and she needs a piece of clothing. Would you help her?"

"Hi Kathryn," the woman said as she stepped forward to Kathryn, holding her hand out in greeting. "Come back here and we will see what we might have," indicating that Kathryn should follow her to their living quarters.

Before going out of the store door into the adobe room, Betsy turned to Ponder and said that he may as well go about his business because, "Kathryn and I have some fitting to do."

Ponder told Knott that he needed to tend to Lilly and to get some things to take to the room. He told Mr. Knott that he could settle for the goods now or for those things and the clothes when Betsy and Kathryn were through. Knott told Ponder to take care of his business and he would have everything ready in a bit and they could settle then.

Going back outside, Ponder released the reins tying Lilly to the post where she had been and walked her across to the house. He took from the saddle, his saddle bags, and the wool blanket and carried those things into the room where he sat them down. Pushing the door to the little house nearly closed, Ponder retrieved the peach can from the saddle bag and took fifty dollars out. He stuck the money in the waist band of his britches. Walking over to the bed, he lifted the mattress at the head and placed the peach can on the slats that held the mattress. Removing his right boot, he recovered the money he carried there and added it to the money he had already placed there from the peach can and put his boot back on. Taking the empty Navy Colt from his bag, he stuck it in the waist of his britches. Fishing around in the saddle bag, he found the flint and placed it by the rock fireplace. Also, he placed the little coffee pot by the fireplace and the one cup he owned on the little table in the room. Remembering his razor, he found it and placed it on nail on the wall by the mirror. Then he laid the saddle bags against the wall.

Going out the door, he took Lilly's reins and led her to the stable behind the trading post and placed her in the pen. He took the saddle, blankets, and bridle on a wooden box that was under the eve of the stable. He walked out of the stable pen, closing the gate behind him. Lilly instantly began to feed on some hay that had been placed there. Carrying the wool blanket, he crossed to the little house and placed it on the foot of the bed inside.

Chapter 19

⊷⇌⊶

Settling In

Leaving the little house again, Ponder headed cross to the trading post. Mr. Knott was standing next to the hitching post with his head down, lighting a pipe that he held between his teeth. Just about the time Ponder came abreast of him, a billow of smoke from the pipe came from his lips.

"Ponder," Mr. Knott said, "Do you know much about this area?"

Ponder replied that he did not.

"Since the war ended, we been blessed with government folk trying to punish us for just being here. If you two stay here as you seem to be planning, you need to know some things. The government people want to make it hard for you to exist here. Then we have outlaws and they want to steal what the government wants to take from you. Thirdly, we have a group that is known as the Mob. The Mob is a vigilante group that wants to hang you if you have been fair with the government people or think you might either be an outlaw or side with them somehow. They have hanged some men around here that I know damned well weren't guilty of anything. Put that in your equation, so to speak, when making a decision. Y'all seem like decent folks and I would hate for you to set your foot into something unexpected.

"Knott, I appreciate your being forthright," said Ponder. "I'm still interested in the places, or at least one of them, that you mentioned earlier. Would either of these places for sale have to do with what you just told me about this area?"

"Both, Ponder," Knott replied.

"Knott," said Ponder, "Make that two boxes each of the cartridges I ordered, if you have them."

Kathryn had been in that room with Betsy what seemed to be a long time. He hadn't heard a commotion, so he figured that woman stuff just took awhile. He crossed back over to the little house, entered, took a chair from the wall, sat down, and removed his boots. Eying the bed, he decided to see if it was more comfortable than the ground he had slept on last night. He laid down and instantly determined that indeed it was. He closed his eyes and just rested, thinking.

No telling how long it was, but the door made a noise and Ponder knew it was opening. Glancing that direction, Kathryn was standing in the light of the door. She was wearing a new, really pretty blue dress. She was beaming as the daylight glistened on and through the edges and ends of her cold, black hair. The way the light was hitting her made it look as if she was standing in front of the brightest light that he had ever seen. She also happened to be the most beautiful thing that he had ever seen. Stepping inside the house and taking the chair that Ponder had taken from the wall, she pulled it to the side of the bed where Ponder lay. Stepping in front of the chair, she sat and then laid her head on the bed directly beside Ponder's head.

She said, "Thank you, Ponder. I love you."

Feeling her in his heart, he turned his head to her and, looking into her eyes, he replied, "Kathryn, I love you too."

Kathryn leaned forward, raising her head a bit, and kissed him gently on his lips. Kathryn asked Ponder if he wanted her to find out from Mr. Knott where the German woman lived that fixed meals. She told him that she could take some money and maybe bring back a meal for them.

"I would appreciate you doing that, we could sit in our room and eat," said Ponder.

Ponder told her that there was money is hidden in his right boot. Kathryn took the money and headed to the trading post to find out where the German woman lived. She was soon on her way to get them something to eat.

While Kathryn was gone, Ponder fetched his razor from the wall peg and, pouring himself some water into a basin, shaved the stubble from his face. The mirror made shaving a bit easier to do. After washing his face and drying it, he went to the porch, pulling a chair with him, and sat down.

Just after Ponder sat down in the chair on the porch, a buggy carrying a man and woman came down the dirt street and stopped at Knott's trading post.

Both people got out of the wagon and went into Knott's store. In a short while, Mr. Knott came out of the store with the man that had been driving the buggy and walked across to where Ponder sat. As they approached, Ponder stood.

"Frederick, this is Ponder," Knott said, as Frederick extended his hand to Ponder.

Ponder reached forward, took Frederick's hand, and shook it. Ponder could tell by Frederick's hand that he was a working man. His hands were calloused and his grip was strong.

"Nice to meet you Frederick," said Ponder. "Pardon me for not having my boots on, I was just relaxing a bit."

"Never you worry, young man. It is nice to make your acquaintance," said Frederick. "Mr. Knott tells me that you might have interest in a place between here and Fredericksburg."

"I do in fact Frederick," said Ponder.

"There is a place about halfway between here and Fredericksburg," said Frederick. "The Ingles have been on it for about fifteen years. They started their endeavor a bit late in life and of late have had a problem living out there. Mr. Ingles fell on some rocks, hurting his leg and hip, and is no longer able to do the work on the place. They have decided to sell the place and move into a house in Fredericksburg. I am thinking that the place is about a section and has a stone house on it and a barn. The house is rock and is of good size, as is the barn. The house backs up against a mountain and there is a spring there that provides water for them. There is a clearing of sorts where Ingles raised corn, mostly for cattle feed. He has a few head of cows, but I don't know the count. It's a typical farm for this area."

"Do you have any idea what the Ingles are asking for the place Frederick?" asked Ponder. "It might be more than what I can bargain for."

"If my memory hasn't failed me Ponder," replied Frederick, "Mr. Ingles is asking one thousand, four hundred, and fifty dollars for the place. It's been for sale for a while. There's few people with that cash these days and the banks are not willing to lend that much. These are not very good economic times around here. If you are truly looking to buy a place, it would be worth your time to consider this place. If you are interested, I can give you the directions.

"The Ingles have already moved off the place and are staying in Fredericksburg with their son Joseph. Joseph has been staying on at the place most days a week, tending the place and making sure that the outlaws don't drive what cattle there is off. The place is fairly easy to find Ponder," said Frederick. "Just cross the bridge and take the road south out from there. About five miles out there is a fork, take the fork to the right. There is going to be a big, red-colored rock mountain on your right. Follow the road along that and take the next fork to the left. In about ten more miles you will come to a creek. turn left along that creek and follow it about a mile to a canyon of sorts. If you keep looking to your left you should see the Ingles' house, back against a small mountain."

Taking Fredericks hand, Ponder shook it and told him thank you.

Frederick's wife came out the door of the store with Betsy Knott. She and Betsy both had store items in their arms which they placed in the back of the buggy.

Frederick turned to walk the few feet to the buggy and turned, saying, "Joseph won't be on the place until three days from now, so you might wait until then to ride there. Also, if you are interested, Joseph can make the deal with you. Now, if you decide to buy it, you will have to come into Fredericksburg to sign the state deed."

"Thanks again Frederick," replied Ponder. This sounded good to him.

Turning to walk back over to the little house, Ponder saw Kathryn walking down the dirt street with a large tray covered with a cloth in her arms. Her new blue dress was bouncing side to side from her movement. Her long black hair was drifting back and forth with her walk, just as her dress was.

She looked like a very happy, proud woman. Ponder was proud for her. Ponder was also proud for himself because his feelings for this woman were something that he had never experienced in his entire life.

Chapter 20

⋆⟩⟨⋆

Dining in Llano

Ponder met Kathryn in front of the porch and took the tray from her. Kathryn stepped onto the porch and into the little house, turning and with a childish smile asked Ponder if he would rather his meal inside the house or on the porch. Kathryn took the tray from Ponder and turning placed it on the bed.

Ponder stood still for a moment, placing his left forefinger against his left cheek as if he was in thought and replied, "I think that I would prefer to eat inside this evening ma'am."

Kathryn then pulled the table away from the wall a bit, gathered the two chairs from the pegs on the wall that held them, and placed one on each side of the table. Turning to the tray on the bed and reaching beneath the cloth, produced two knives and forks which she prudently placed on each side of the table. Then taking Ponders hand, she led him the short step to the table. Pulling that chair out, she asked Ponder if he would please be seated and she sat him down.

Again from the tray, she produced two honest to goodness glasses, each filled with what appeared to be water. Then two ceramic plates, that she also placed at each side. Next came a small platter with what appeared to be a large piece of roasted beef with gravy on it, and a batch of potatoes, fried with onions mixed in it. Also, there was a small cloth holding four pieces of fresh bread.

Then, taking the cloth that had covered the meal in transit and placing it over her left forearm, Kathryn walked to the side of Ponder and in a horrible German accent said, "Sir, I cannot pronounce what we are having for supper."

79

She leaned forward to the face of the guy smiling at her and quickly kissed his lips. She then went to her chair and was sat herself. Beyond where Kathryn was Ponder could see the tray that the food had been carried on and there were two pieces of what appeared to be apple pie sitting on the tray. Looking then at Kathryn, Ponder wondered to himself what the hell Albert had thought he was doing.

Then across the table Kathryn reached for Ponder's hands and, holding them firmly, said, "This looks good, doesn't it?" and they both laughed. "That woman, Mrs. Ooric, Ulric, Ulrick, whatever her name is, speaks about as much English as I do German. Sweet woman! She evidently lost her husband. Must be sixty or so years old. She just talked and talked and talked to me. She shook her finger at me a few times. She would laugh and slap her side, I like her. I actually think that she liked me being there. Very clean person, very clean place. That was fun."

He was glad that it had been fun for Kathryn. He hardly knew what exactly fun meant, because he didn't remember ever having any. What was happening at this very moment seemed to be about as much fun as he had ever had. If this was "fun" he would like to have it every day, from now on.

Finishing their meal, Kathryn, gathered the dishes and utensils and placed them on the tray that had been provided to bring the meal to the little house. The two plates that had held the pieces of apple pie looked as if they had already been washed, it had been so good. Kathryn left the house with the tray and walked back to the lady's home that had prepared it.

The lady when answering the door said something in German and Kathryn responded that he had loved it which caused the woman to cross her arms over her chest with delight. Kathryn told her that she would help clean the dishes up and the woman put her hands down and made a movement like she was moving chickens and was saying "shoo, shoo," pointing at the house where Ponder was.

It was late evening. It had been a full day. A good day, but a full one as well. Ponder had gotten some coffee from Knott and made a pot of coffee in their little fireplace. They sat on the porch, even in darkness, drinking the coffee and Ponder relayed the information about the place that Frederick had told him about while standing in front of Knott's store prior to Kathryn arriving with their meal. It all sounded exciting to Kathryn. She had a lot of questions that, as of now, Ponder had no answer for. He simply told her that they would have to go look at the place. Ponder said that it sounded good, but he still wanted to see how it was put together. The Texas stars came out and again in the darkness Ponder could see the reflection of them in Kathryn's eyes.

Soon, the pot was rinsed as well as the cups and they were placed by the fireplace. The door and windows were closed and a candle was lit just long enough for them to get undressed for bed. When Kathryn was safely in bed, Ponder blew the flame from the candle and placed it on the table with a match nearby in case they need get up that night. Again, Kathryn got on her elbow to raise herself and kissed Ponder on his lips before laying flat and getting so close to him it was like they were one.

But before going to sleep, Kathryn said very softly, "Ponder? What is the minister for?"

Ponder responded by lightly squeezing the hand that was wrapped over his chest.

Chapter 21

⊷⟞⊙⟝⊷

'The' Day Comes

Ponder was awake just enough to realize that the sun was up. A ray of light passed through the divide in one of the shutters and was illuminating the room somewhat. He had felt Kathryn move slightly, but being the first in several nights that she slept on something other than a saddle blanket for padding, he figured that she had slept well and was comfortable, too comfortable to get up. Besides, she had no wood to gather, nor fires to start, nor blankets to fold so her excuse was good, even though she had not used it.

Ponder heard a footstep on the wooden porch and quickly slid his britches and shirt on. There was a light tap or two on the front door and Ponder opened it slightly to see who it was. Knott was standing there.

He said, "Ponder, that Minister just rode in and I told him that you might want to see him. He will be waiting in the store."

"Thanks Mr. Knott," replied Ponder. "I will be there as soon as I can straighten my hair and get my boots on."

In a matter of a few minutes, Ponder was crossing the path between Knott's store and the little house. He saw the man that was obviously the Minister standing inside the store.

As he entered, Knott said to the Minister, "Reverend Clark, this is Ponder, the man that asked me about a Minister."

To which Ponder extended his hand to shake the Minister's. Reverend Clark asked what it was that he was needed for. Imagining what the Minister was going to think about what he was going to say, Ponder told him that there

83

was a lady in that little house across the way and that he would like the Reverend to marry them. Reverend Clark gently took Ponder by his arm and led him out of the trading post.

"Son," said Reverend Clark, "Are you already living with this woman?"

"We met along the trail coming this direction a few days ago. She was frightened and starving. We quickly became comfortable around one another. I had one blanket and, yes, we have slept under it and that's all. I am ready to settle down on some property and I am wanting this woman, Kathryn, to marry me and be with me. I am asking you to marry us."

Reverend Clark inquired as to when he would like for this to take place and Ponder's answer was right now, an hour from now, this afternoon, but sometime this day.

"Do you have any idea where you want to do this?" asked Reverend Clark.

Ponder pointed at a huge live oak just behind the little house a way, "How about beneath that oak, Reverend? I am hoping that our marriage will be as strong as it and last as long."

"Would about eleven o'clock work for you?" asked Reverend Clark.

"It would," replied Ponder, "And by the way, what day of the year is this?"

Reverend Clark replied, "It is October second, in the year 1870 A.D."

Ponder shook the Reverend's hand again and walked toward Knott's store. He stopped, looked back at Reverend Clark, and said, "See you at eleven o'clock."

Then he walked into the dim store and was looking everywhere for something to fashion a ring from. Knott stood there laughing and asking Ponder what in the name of God was he looking for.

Ponder replied, "A ring."

"Oh!" replied Knott and they both started looking.

The opening of boxes, sliding of drawers, and chatter between Knott and Ponder eventually got Knott's wife Betsy curious and she stepped from the adobe room into the store and asked what in the world was going on.

"Oh!" said Betsy excitedly and soon she was doing the same as they. Within minutes, the German woman that cooked meals for them walked in the trading post door. Olga Ulrich, was what her name was, Ponder learned after Betsy answered Ponder's question about her name. Olga was trying to figure out what the fuss was about with the three of them seemingly desperately looking for something. Neither Betsy nor Knott understood or spoke German, so Betsy held up two little spikes in the shape of a cross, took Ponder's hand, and walked down an aisle in the store making him walk together with her right up to Knott, who acted as if he was holding a book with both hands. Betsy then rubbed her fingers up and down her own left ring finger and Olga then totally understood the dilemma. Olga turned as if being chased and took off out the trading post door and was nearly running in the direction of her home.

The trio were still looking for something from which to fashion a ring. In moments, a panting Olga showed back up at the trading post door, stepped in and in front of Ponder, took his hand and opened it, placing in his palm a golden wedding band. It was somewhat worn, but still beautiful. Ponder was astonished! This had to be this lady's wedding ring. He thanked her softly and opened her hand and placed the ring back in her hand.

"I know that you don't understand what I am saying, but I cannot let you do this," said Ponder softly.

Touching her heart with her other hand and, with a tear in her eye, she held her palm out again to Ponder saying something like "please".

With this, Ponder was even more taken aback than before. He pointed at the house where Kathryn was and at the ring and then back at Olga indicating that she should give the ring. Olga understood. Grasping the ring tightly in her palm, she turned and left, walking back to her home. Ponder truly hoped that she understood, but even then found a piece of wire and cut it in a short piece, fashioning a ring, and placed it in his coat pocket.

In a short while, Ponder returned to the house to find Kathryn putting her clothes on. "Gosh Ponder, I haven't slept like that since I can't remember," said Kathryn.

"I did the same," said Ponder. "Must have been that supper we had or possibly that bed. It's way more comfortable than any ground I ever slept on."

"Hard ground, soft bed, it makes no difference," said Kathryn, "So long as you are there."

Ponders heart was in his throat. He did not know whether to ask the seriousness of her being his and use the answer to ask her to marry him at eleven o'clock or not. *What if I walk her to that tree at two o'clock and she tells me "I'm not quite that serious, Ponder"?* He decided to walk her to the tree. He suspected that seeing a man standing there with a bible in his hand might be a good clue to her of what was about to happen.

In a short while, Olga Ulrich was at their door. She had a tray in her hand that had a pair of sweet rolls and two glasses of what turned out to be apple cider in them. Olga smiled at Kathryn and Kathryn went to the door, took the tray, and handed it to Ponder. She then turned and hugged Olga like a good relative or maybe a mother. Kathryn was beaming as was Olga, who turned and stepped from the porch and headed to her house with what seemed a slight skip in her step.

Ponder moved the table to the porch and there they ate the rolls and drank the cider that Olga had brought them. It was very good, unlike dried meat and coffee which just got you by.

Ponder was so ready to be "somewhere" soon and live like a person with a place to be. For age twenty-one, he was tired of life as he had lived it. The money from the drive and the woman sitting on the porch with him were his chance for that.

Ponder had noticed a bit of activity in Llano this morning. There had been several people showed up in wagons or on horseback and had either gone into the trading post and came out with typical supplies or they were just milling around, shaking hands and seemingly visiting. He and Kathryn enjoyed sitting on the porch even though it was a rented one. They talked a bit about the feeling of being part of a community. Kathryn knew this experience, but Ponder had never had the opportunity. The strength of this country and this area did not depend on an army or a government, it depended on people much like these that prop one another up.

A little time passed and there was the sound of a fiddle being played somewhere nearby. Both he and Kathryn were trying to name the songs and words that might go with them. The music got a bit louder or closer and a few people were drifting past their little house headed some place to the side and behind them. Finally, with curiosity taking its course, they got up and looked in the direction the noise was coming from and the music as well.

Standing under the live oak that Ponder had chosen to be married to Kathryn under, was Knott. He was playing a violin. Others were standing beneath the tree laughing and visiting. Ponder noticed Reverend Clark walking from the trading post across to the live oak. It was only a moment before Betsy, Knott's wife, walked up and asked them to come join in. They both were already standing and walked, following Betsy toward the live oak. As they reached the area, the little crowd parted to let them walk through. Ponder thought it must be eleven o'clock. Reverend Clark motioned for them to come closer to him in the group of folks gathered there and they did.

From the group, Olga Ulrich stepped out and walked to Kathryn. She had a large, very fine white scarf that she folded in half and placed on Kathryn's head.

Reverend Clark said, "Ponder, is something you wish to say?"

Ponder placed his hands in Kathryn's and said, "Kathryn, I love you. I wish to spend my time on earth with you. Will you marry me?"

Kathryn, caught totally off guard, nearly jumped into Ponder's arms and told him, "I am yours and I wish to be your wife, forever."

The Reverend stepped into the crowd and, taking each gently by their arms, escorted them to the base of the huge live oak. From the corner of his eye he could see someone moving up beside him. Kathryn did not have to see from the corner of her eye because Olga Ulrich stood just behind and to the side of Ponder with a piece of cloth with a golden ring pinned to it. Kathryn was just about shining. She had tears on her face but an everlasting smile on her lips. The words were said, the questions asked, the ring unpinned and placed on Kathryn's ring finger. Then the I do's, a kiss, a cheer from a crowd of strangers, and they were man and wife. Ponder's normal height was five foot seven or eight inches, but at this moment he was ten feet tall.

It seemed that the church congregation went from a church service to a wedding reception. They all moved from beneath the live oak to the dirt road that passed by the trading post and then by the little house. Knott followed them all, still playing his fiddle but his music changed from hymnal music to a lively jig-type program. It wasn't long before another visitor to town and the church service produced a guitar and, between he and Knott, everyone in the street was dancing with somebody. Kathryn pulled Ponder's face close to her's using both of her arms and kissed him. It was not a "peck" as some judged kisses. After doing so, she whispered in Ponder's ear that he had made her happier than she had ever been in her life. Then backing her head away to where they were nose to nose, she told him that they were going to have a wonderful life. Ponder really didn't know what to say. He too was happy because Kathryn was, in fact, now his.

Ponder took Kathryn in his arms and danced with her as best he could to the tune of the music. Almost every man, woman, and child present danced with Kathryn. Ponder danced with perhaps every woman there and a couple of little girls that first seemed too shy to dance. For certain, Ponder found Olga, hugged her, kissed her on her cheek, and danced with her.

Before the sun began to set, most everyone climbed back into or on what brought them to church that day and headed back to where they had come from. They were all simple, hard-working, very nice people. All of them, every single one, came by before leaving and wished Ponder and Kathryn the best of luck and said how nice it would be if they lived in the area. If they managed to find a place to buy, and the one that the Frederick people are selling sure sounded like it would fit the bill, he hoped that in time he and Kathryn would indeed know all of these people.

Chapter 22

⋅→☰◉☰←⋅

And Night as Well

With the area empty of the people now and the sun beginning to set, Kathryn laid herself back against Ponder as they stood on the porch of the little house. Ponder had his arms around the front of Kathryn.

Ponder said, "This is hard for me to believe Kathryn. Before you showed up, all I had were a mess of dreams that I hoped would come true. I have wished for a long time to have someone and a place for me and that someone to share. Maybe have a family. You know, a real life, and know where I will be the next day and the months and years after that. Then suddenly things happened that moved me that direction and that all started with you. I pray that this is what you want Kathryn."

Turning within Ponder's arms, Kathryn replied, "Ponder, I learned all about you that I ever need to know within an hour of seeing you for the first time. You are what I was dreaming of when I was just a child, dreaming of growing into womanhood. Ponder, as well as you know, I do have a past, but you are never going to realize it." With that, Kathryn loosened her arm on one side of Ponder and walked him from the little porch and into the little house.

Once inside, Ponder closed the door. He also lighted the candle and sat it on the table. The shutters were already closed. Everything outside was quiet. Kathryn removed her shoes and her clothes. Except for the gold ring on her finger, she was naked. She had never been bothered about Ponder seeing her with nothing on, but this time it seemed different. There was a way about her that made everything seem new when it really wasn't. Kathryn then came to

89

Ponder and had him sit while she removed his boots. Then she pulled him to his feet and slowly removed his clothing, a piece at a time. She embraced him and gave him a kiss, much different than those she had given him before. They stood, kissed, and felt one another's bodies for some time in the flickering candle light, looking into each other's eyes.

She then turned, got on the foot of the bed kneeling, and motioned Ponder to come to the bed and do the same at the head of the bed, facing her. She then took his hands in hers and she told him that she wanted him to know her, everything about her. She then released his hands.

Ponder raised his hands to the sides of her face and ran his fingers gently up the sides of her head against her scalp, letting her cold black soft hair slip between his fingers. With his fingers against the sides of her head, he gently and slowly ran his thumbs from above her nose tracing the outline of her eyebrows. His middle fingers felt the outline of her nose as they found her lips, which he also traced with his index fingers. Embracing her, his hand went to her back where he felt the depression that her spine laid in and he felt the scars from the razor strop she carried now. He rubbed the scars gently as if to make them go away. He felt of her wrists and those parts leading to her shoulders which gently sloped to her beautiful neck.

At the down towards her breast, he hesitated slightly. Kathryn, noticing the hesitation, took his hands and led them to her breast and then released her hold. Ponder slowly, and as gently as possible, cupped the outline of Kathryn's breast. He felt of the roundness and firmness of them and, having never felt a woman's breast before, was amazed at how soft yet firm they felt. Then to her nipples, which seemed to be harder than the rest of the breast. He placed his thumbs in the center of her stomach, just below her breast, and used his fingers to feel the sides of her as he moved his hands downward. He eventually placed his hands on every part of Kathryn's body. For Ponder, it was a true learning experience as he had never had his hands on any part of any woman. It was wonderful.

Kathryn did much the same in her exploration of Ponder. He also had some scars and she dwelled on them a bit. She too, left no part unexplored with her getting to know her new husband. With that, Kathryn laid Ponder on his back and laid herself on top of him, engulfing him with kisses.

"I truly am yours Ponder," she said lovingly. From there, she mounted Ponder holding his hands with hers above his head. "You truly are mine as well," said Kathryn.

The marriage was consummated. All the while, Ponder could see the light from the dim flickering candle reflecting in Kathryn's eyes. The fire in her body was much greater than the light from the candle. He had no idea it would be like this.

Morning came and the two were still entwined in one another's arms, even in sleep.

Chapter 23

⊷⟾ ⟾⊷

And the First Day

It was Kathryn who stirred first. She playfully wiggled against Ponder and then swung her feet to the floor. She stood, stretched for a moment, and slipped a dress on before going to take a look out the door. While opening the door, bright sunlight hit her and she squinted because of its brightness. Looking down she saw a tray, covered with a cloth, on which two huge pastry rolls sat on a plate beside a large bottle of what was most likely apple juice.

"Oh!" she said, "This is wonderful." She looked to see if Olga was already out of sight, and she was.

Picking the tray up carefully, she turned back through the door and told Ponder that he would not believe what that sweet woman has done "She brought us two gorgeous sweet rolls for breakfast and some more of her cider."

"Good Lord that sounds good," replied Ponder.

Kathryn unloaded the tray on the table as quickly. As soon as Ponder could get clothes on he was in the second chair with one of the fresh rolls and was savoring every bite.

"My goodness this is good," said Ponder.

"I wish I could get Olga to show me how to make these things, Germans are the best at this," said Kathryn.

Over their breakfast, Ponder asked Kathryn if she would like to go for a ride.

"Might be fun Ponder. Anyplace special?" she said.

"Thought we would go see if we can find the Ingles' place. Their son sup-posedly is there today. Figured we could take a look and talk about it and if

93

you are interested we will see if we can buy it. How does that sound?" Ponder said.

"Then it would wonderful, more than fun Ponder," said Kathryn. "This is all unbelievable."

Ponder put his hat on and gathered up his Navy and head out the door, stopping for moment to ask Kathryn if she could ride a horse. "Yes, I can," was the reply.

He walked into Knott's store and asked if he might have a horse and rigging to rent for the day and maybe part of tomorrow morning.

"I do," said Knott.

"I would like to rent it then Mr. Knott. Also," said Ponder, "I would like one of the boxes of .36 paper cartridges and some caps for it, as well as one of the boxes of Flat Henry's."

"Done," said Knott as he laid the items on the counter.

Opening the paper cartridges, he squeezed six of them into the Navy and capped five cylinders, "I would be happy to pay what I owe you right now if you wish, Mr. Knott."

"We'll get it before you folks leave here Ponder," said Knott.

Ponder left the Navy and the two boxes of cartridges laying on the counter and asked Knott which horse he should saddle. Ponder headed to the corral and stood with Lilly for a bit, just talking and making do over her, and then saddled her. Knott walked around the corner and told Ponder to saddle the gray for Kathryn, which he did. Then he led both mounts to the front of the little house and tied then to the post. Kathryn stuck her head out the door and asked if she needed to bring the saddlebags and Henry.

Ponder said, "Yes and throw the can of peaches in the saddlebag if you will."

In just a minute, Kathryn came out the door with an armload of what Ponder had asked for. He placed the saddle bag on Lilly and the Henry in the scabbard. Kathryn looked a lot like an excited child. She had also thought to gather the little pot and flint and had placed them in the saddle bag along with the peaches. Ponder knew better than to ask what she had packed. Together they led Lilly and Knott's horse across to the store. Ponder entered, picked up his Navy, and stuck it in his waist along with two boxes of cartridges and the tin of caps he carried out and placed in the saddle bag. At this point, the only thing Kathryn wasn't doing was jumping up and down and clapping her hands.

"Kathryn," Ponder said, "Go in and get us something to eat in case we are late getting back or have to stay overnight."

In a moment, out the door she came with canned beans, peaches, and canned beef, plus a straw hat on her head. Which she turned several times, showing it off, "I had Knott put this on our bill."

Ponder thought about the "our bill" thing and laughed. Ponder helped Kathryn mount the rented horse and away they went, following the directions given to the Ingles' place. By the sun, Ponder figured the trip had taken about three hours. It was pretty country and a nice ride for them both. They got to talk a lot. As the directions had said, they reached the creek that was described, turned to their left and very quickly could see the Ingles' place.

Ponder pulled up, dismounted, and pulled the Navy from his waist and placed it in the saddle bag. Remounting, they rode on to the gated fence around the house. The house looked to be about thirty by maybe fifty feet in size and must have a loft because the rook seemed high. To the left was what appeared to be a nice barn with a corral attached. A few implements were resting along one side of it. There was a small attachment on the side of the house towards the barn which Ponder guessed was a place to cook. It had one chimney and the house had two. Just behind the attachment was what he guessed was a smokehouse, based on how it was constructed. The house and smokehouse were made of stone, as were the lower walls of the barn.

"Hello the house," called Ponder.

In short time, a man appeared at the door asking what they needed.

"My name is Ponder and this is my wife Kathryn," he said, "I met a Mr. Frederick in Llano that said this place might be for sale. He said that you would be the son of the owner, Mr. Ingles."

With that, the man walked out and through the gate and extended his hand to Ponder saying, "I am Joseph Ingles."

Ponder explained what Mr. Frederick had told him about his father's misfortune.

"What Frederick has told you is true Ponder. This place is six hundred and forty acres, but about thirty percent of it is uphill rock and, aside from scenery or wind break, serves no useful purpose. There is a field that you passed coming in that has been cultivated to grow grains, mostly for the cattle. The barn is a fine one. I can show you the house, barn, and then the property markers if you wish."

"Been on a horse for a few hours, Joseph. Let's walk around and see the buildings first."

"Let's start with the house Mr. and Mrs. Ponder."

Ponder started to say something, but did not and they walked through the gate and under the porch and into the house. Ponder noticed that the rock walls were at least two and a half feet thick. The room had a dining area toward the attached room which did turn out to be a kitchen. Across from the dining area was a counter with a metal sink in it. Joseph noted that there was a pipe from that wall to the spring on the mountain just behind the house. The other direction from the front door were two rooms used as bedrooms. One of these had a fireplace in it with a hearth that opened to both downstairs rooms. Up the wall, dividing the living area and the bedrooms, was a stair case with a very gentle incline and handrail that went to a loft that was divided into two rooms. It curved around the chimney on the fireplace on that end of the room. Glancing at Kathryn, Ponder asked what she thought.

Her answer was, "It's beautiful Ponder."

Joseph told them that the furniture stayed with the house. The place his parents had moved into was rather small and they did not need the furnishings from here. They then headed out the door and to the right to where the barn stood. The barn matched the house, it was a nice, sturdy barn with thick stone walls at the bottom of the structure.

"I can show you the smokehouse if you wish to see it Ponder," said Joseph.

"No need," said Ponder, "I'm sure it is in order."

Joseph then added that his parents no longer need the stock on the place so everything goes with the place, including the wagon. Ponder inquired how much stock he was talking about.

"Well," said Joseph, "There are nineteen head of cattle and a milk cow. There are two goats my mother used for milk for making cheese. There are two draft horses for the implements and two horses for riding, plus four dozen chickens or more." Joseph said that was about all he could tell them about the living area and asked if they wanted to see the out property now.

"That would be fine," Ponder said. He inquired of Kathryn if she wished to stay there or see the property. Kathryn wanted to ride with them. She wanted to see everything.

Joseph saddled his horse and led them around the property line except where it went up steep sides of the mountain. Joseph pointed out that each corner of the property had a stone with an "I" carved into it. They rode back to the house.

"What do you folks think?" asked Joseph.

There was no need to ask Kathryn that question. Ponder imagined that she thought she would never see better, plus it was everything. They needed to do nothing but live there and work the property.

"Mr. Ingles," Ponder inquired, "What are you asking for this place?"

"Ponder," said Joseph, "We think the place is worth a lot more than what we will take for it. No one has the money these days so, although we have had two parties look at it, they made no offer. We would like to have one thousand, four hundred, and fifty dollars for it. We don't want to finance it and would prefer cash."

"Joseph," Ponder admitted, "I have never owned property in my life. I know nothing of what needs to be done in a sale of a place like this."

Joseph told him that if he wished to buy the place, after payment, he could write a bill of sale representing his father. At some point, Ponder would need to come to Fredericksburg to register the bill of sale to get a title. Looking at Kathryn, Ponder asked once more what she thought.

"It's a long way from town, but it looks like us Ponder," stated Kathryn.

Ponder walked to where Lilly stood, standing on her off side he took the peach can from the saddlebag and counted out the amount Joseph mentioned. Walking back to Joseph and Kathryn, Ponder counted out the fifteen hundred dollars that Joseph had proposed and handed it to him. Joseph suggested that they go in the house and a bill of sale would be signed and dated. Joseph told them that he would stay the night, but would vacate the next morning and the house would be ready for them the next night if need be. Joseph stood and told them since the sale was done that there was one more thing he wished for them to see. Walking to the fireplace, he gathered an 'L' shaped tool and walked back to the area near where the table sat. Turning the tool through a small hole in the oaken floor, he pulled up on the tool and a door in the floor opened. It was a very large cellar.

"Storage and safety," said Joseph, with Ponder and Kathryn looking into the cellar.

Chapter 24

⊷⊜⊶

Plans

After a short farewell with Joseph, Ponder and Kathryn mounted their horses and headed back to Llano. In seeing the Ingles' place, which was now theirs, Kathryn was seeing all the dreams that she ever had come true. Being so taken so with Ponder in such a short time seemed preposterous, but it had meant to be. Ponder was thinking that just a few days ago, aside from the cattle money, he had nothing. Now it seemed as if he had everything and it had all been delivered in one bundle. Neither even thought about stopping along the way back to Llano and eating. They just rode along having short conversations about their new home. Mid-afternoon they pulled up to Knott's store and dismounted. Ponder realized that he had not even taken the Navy from the saddlebag to make the trip back to Llano.

Ponder led both horses around to the corral, removed all the trappings from them, and made sure there was some feed out for them as well. With the Henry in hand and saddle bags over his shoulder, he walked around to the front of Knott's. Kathryn was giving Mr. Knott and Betsy a detailed item for item description of the "Ponder" place. She was still very excited, Ponder was also. Ponder explained the details to the Knott's much like Kathryn had done.

Knott commented that he would probably not have looked at anything else either. Ponder told him that they would pull out and head back to the place in the morning. He also thanked them for their help and friendship.

"Me too," said Kathryn and she gave Mr. Knott a big hug and kissed him on the cheek. And then, looking at Betsy, she said, "You have been so wonderful to me" and stepped forward and hugged Betsy also.

Ponder also told the Knott's that once settled, they might start riding in and attend church on Sundays with Reverend Clark, "When we settle what we owe you, I would like to leave a few dollars that you might give the Reverend. I intended to do it yesterday but I sort of forgot about it."

"Gladly," said Knott. "We kind of hate to see you kids leave. This is the most excitement I can ever remember in Llano."

While Kathryn was still talking excitedly with Betsy, Ponder went to the house and set the saddlebag and Henry down. It dawned on him that they were going to have to return soon, either to Llano or to Fredericksburg, and get staples. They would need the wagon for that. *We're going to need more than a can of beans and some peaches*, thought Ponder.

Kathryn showed up soon and Ponder inquired if they would have the beans and peaches she bought for supper or did she want to see if Olga could supply something.

"I'd rather ask Olga," said Kathryn.

"Sounds good to me Kathryn. I wish she was going with us tomorrow, she's a good cook."

"And a wonderful person," said Kathryn, glancing at the ring on her finger. She left the house headed for Olga's, but in just a few minutes was back.

She wrapped her arms around Ponder and kissed him, saying, "Gosh! I love you so much. Ponder, Olga is such a sweet woman and obviously has no one, plus she is a wonderful cook. Would you consider asking her to come live with us? It'd be nice having her and who knows, one day we might have children and she would be a blessing to have with us then."

In just a few seconds Ponder told her, "We have plenty of room and she is a good cook. She would be a pleasure to have around. Ask her if you wish."

Another quick kiss on his lips and Kathryn was out the door headed to Knott's where Betsy and Knott tried to teach her, as best they could, how to ask Olga in her own language what she and Ponder had spoken of. In a short while, Kathryn was walking down the street practicing the words taught her by the Knotts.

Arriving at Olga's, and after Olga motioned for her to come in, Kathryn hugged Olga and, holding Olga's hands in hers, said clumsily "Wis willstdu von mir leben bei uns."

Standing there for a moment, Olga was trying to decide what Kathryn was attempting to say to her. Then it dawned on her Kathryn's intent. Her mouth opened a bit as one hand left Kathryn's and went to cover it. She then gently grabbed Kathryn's shoulders with her hands and began to cry softly. She then pointed at herself and Kathryn only knew to shake her head yes. Olga's hands came together in front of her face as if praying and shook her head "yes".

Olga took Kathryn to her stove and took the lid from the pot on it. Seemed like supper tonight would be what looked like chicken and dumplings.

"See you this evening," said Kathryn to Olga and she headed back to the little house. "I was talking to Knott and settling what we owe him and told him about maybe taking Olga to live with us." Kathryn was loving the word "we". "He seemed glad that Olga was going with us and for her to have something like a family. I'll help move her Ponder. Knott is even going to help us load Olga's things and is carrying them to our place tomorrow. We are going to somehow convey to Olga that she needs to buy some supplies from for us before we leave. I'll see if Mrs. Knott will tell her that. She speaks a bit of German."

Chapter 25

＊━◯⊂━＊

Last Night in Llano

By the time Kathryn went to Olga's to pick up their supper, Olga was jovial and excited. Supper was placed on the tray and Kathryn headed back to the house with it. She told Olga that she would be back with the tray of dishes and wash them, but she thought it doubtful that Olga understood. Back to the house she went.

Ponder was already at the table and gruffly grumbled at her while lightly pounding fist on the table asking, "Where is my supper woman?"

Setting the tray on the table and wagging her finger at him, she told him that if he was bad he would have to go to bed without any supper, "You probably won't even like these old chicken and dumplings anyway."

"Kathryn," said Ponder, "If they taste half as good as they smell they might be the best thing we have ever eaten."

Kathryn commented that Olga was so excited about leaving tomorrow with us that she couldn't sit still. The chicken and dumplings were devoured. Kathryn gathered the dishes and utensils and headed out the door headed to Olga's to help her clean up. In a short while she was back, telling Ponder that Olga was already packing her belongings to leave in the morning. Ponder was sitting on the chair where he had sat for supper. Kathryn closed and latched the front door and willfully stood in front of Ponder, undressing very slowly. After placing her clothes on the other chair, she knelt in front of Ponder and carefully removed his boots and then his coat, shirt, and britches. With Ponder standing, she embraced him as if she was becoming a part of his body. He placed his arms under her, picked her up, and laid her on the bed.

"You might consider sleeping on the floor tonight," she said in a rough voice. "If you think Olga is excited, wait until you see how excited I am. I'm going to love you to death."

By the time the evening was over and they went to sleep, he determined he was ready to face death any time Kathryn wanted to offer it.

Chapter 26

⊷⥱ ⥲⊶

Going Home

At just after daylight, Kathryn arose as if an alarm had gone off, dressed quickly, kissed Ponder on the lips gently, and was gone out the door. He got up slowly and started dressing in anticipation of the busy morning ahead with loading Olga, her belongings, and some supplies into Knott's wagon. He was trying to think of how to convey to Olga that he wanted her to pick out all the supplies that he had on hand to take to their house. He was hoping that Betsy could explain it to her.

It wasn't five minutes until Kathryn was back to the room, carrying a tray with what he knew was breakfast on it. This morning it was scrambled eggs with a cheese mixed in them and some toasted bread plus two glasses, again, of the cider. They were quick to eat it with Ponder exclaiming to Kathryn that if he wasn't careful Olga was going to make him fat fast.

Before they could even finish breakfast, Knott was at the door telling him that the wagon was ready and he would meet him at Olga's when they were finished eating. He did not get to finish, as a matter of fact because Kathryn, stood and scooped the plates from the table, placing them back on the tray and, with it in hand, headed to Olga's.

"Guess I better get to moving," Ponder said to himself, laughing.

While walking to Olga's, Ponder was overcome by Betsy Knott. She told him how nice it was of them to include Olga, as she had no one any longer.

He took a moment to tell her, "I have asked that she buy everything that she thinks we will need from you folks before we leave."

105

"I think that is a smart idea Ponder. I will make her understand what you want. Might be hard for her to do that because she is so used to just making do. I will help her as best I can. Kathryn told us about everything that is being left there by the Ingles. Are there covers on the beds?"

"I don't recall any Betsy, just mattresses," Ponder replied. "Pretty sure they would have taken that sort of stuff."

Betsy took Ponders arms, causing him to stop and she faced him, "You folks are the brightest light we have seen here in a very long time. Most that we see are the people that are hardened from these times. That wife of yours is like a flickering candle that is about to turn into a bright flame." Placing her finger against his chest she told him that he had better take good care of her.

"Mrs. Knott," he replied, "I have every intention of doing just that."

"Do you know much about Kathryn?" she asked.

"No ma'am, I don't," he said. "She showed up five days ago and you see where we are now."

"We would like to ride out sometime and see you young people Ponder," said Betsy. "We think that you two have sort of become a part of us."

"Betsy," Ponder said, "I can think of nothing that I would like better that for y'all to come and see us. I assure you that Kathryn would say the same. I'm telling you Betsy, I am thinking that we were going nowhere without Olga. I never had a family, so being close to people is a new adventure for me. It's nearly like Kathryn had the same life."

"Not sure she didn't," replied Betsy.

Ponder thought about that.

Walking again, they were at Olga's place. Between Olga and Kathryn, most all of Olga's few belongings were stacked neatly in front of the house where she had been living. Olga's face showed red cheeks and a happy smile. Kathryn, still excited by what was happening, had worked up a bit of a sweat and had a few strands of her black hair stuck to her forehead. She ran forth to Ponder and hugged him, for nothing but just to do so. She stood close to his side for a moment with her arm around his back. It was if he had known her for years, not five days.

Loading Olga's things on the wagon only took a few minutes. She fussed at them about one crate that they knew held her dishes and glasses.

"I think we are ready to go," stated Kathryn, brushing her hands together as if there was dirt or dust on them.

Betsy explained to Olga what Ponder had wished, about buying supplies. Olga went from happy smiling face to a happy business-like face as she was considering what the needs would be.

Pulling the wagon back to the store, Knott gathered a bench that sat against the wall in front of his store and placed it in the wagon for at least two of the women to sit on for the trip. Ponder went to the corral and visited with Lilly for a bit before getting her ready to travel. He walked her over to the little house and gathered the loose things there to place in his saddle bag. Taking the peach can from beneath the mattress, he took a bit of cash and stuck it in his boot and put the can into the saddlebag which he placed on Lilly when he got outside. One more trip inside and he had his Navy and Henry. Outside, he slid the Henry into its scabbard and walked Lilly across to the store.

Olga was walking around the store, telling Betsy what she wanted as Betsy was writing the order on a piece of brown paper. Knott was gathering the things as Betsy wrote them down and set it all just outside the door. Ponder would have placed it in the wagon except Kathryn had already taken that job. She seemed to be in her glory. Walking by Kathryn, Ponder placed the money he had just taken from his boot in her hand. She seemed to not even be paying attention to what he had done but was still involved with the loading of supplies.

Soon, that work was done. Walking in the store, Kathryn asked Olga if she had ordered all we need, which was translated by Betsy to Olga who with a smile said, "Ya".

Kathryn asked Mr. Knott what their bill was and she paid him that amount. He turned to Olga and said, "Let's go home Olga Ulrich."

Olga was out the door and sat on the bench placed in the wagon by Vernon Knott. Soon, Knott was driving the wagon with Betsy beside him and Kathryn was on the bench in the bed with Olga. Ponder followed behind them, headed to the Ponder place.

A few necessary stops were made but according to Knott's timepiece, the trip had taken them two hours and twenty minutes. Ponder had the gate to the property open when the wagon rolled up and went on through to the fence around the house. The three women and Knott climbed from the wagon as Ponder dismounted Lilly and they met at the fence gate.

"This is it," said Kathryn. "This is our new home."

The Knotts responded with, "It's a nice one".

But Olga just stood in amazement, knowing that she too had a home now. Ponder opened the gate and Kathryn led them all to the house and inside. There were ah's from Betsy and Vernon while Olga was just walking around slowly touching everything. At least for now, Kathryn wished to put Olga in one of the downstairs bedrooms. So taking her by the hand, she led Olga to what would be her room. Olga entered the room and turned to look at Kathryn. She had a happy face, but it had tears on it. She hugged and kissed Kathryn and then to Ponder where she did the same. Ponder suggested they get the wagon unloaded and then find something for lunch.

Olga had wandered off into the little kitchen room and, seeing the smokehouse in back, opened the door and went to inspect it. To her delight, there were hams there, wrapped in linen cloth and cured, as she could see the drippings of sooty salt that had formed on the bottoms of the wrapped hams. Returning to the house, she went out front and helped the others unload the wagon. They carried most of what Olga had, which was dishes and cookware to the kitchen and carefully sat it on the floor. The boxes with her few clothes and personal items were taken to the back bedroom at sat next to the bed.

It didn't take much effort to unload things belonging to Kathryn and Ponder because they had so very little. But Ponder brought the saddle bag from Lilly and the Henry from its scabbard and carried those in. He unsaddled Lilly and let her walk free. He would place the saddle and bridle in the barn later.

Olga was back in the house and looking at the cooking area. She really liked it.

Walking back though the living area, she saw the staircase going up beside the fireplace chimney and went up them. The first room had a fireplace with a side chimney that linked with the large one below. The room was a good size and had a door to the other room that would be used for storage most likely. She really liked the big room and it would offer her some privacy and her being up here would also offer Kathryn and Ponder some privacy.

Going back downstairs, she explained what she thought to Becky, who then explained it to Kathryn. Olga's things were then moved upstairs. To Olga, it seemed like it was her own little home within the house.

Then back down the stairs came Olga. Going to the kitchen, she built a fire in the big kitchen stove. She found a few potatoes that they had purchased at Knott's store and peeled them, placed them in a pot of water with a bit of salt, and began to boil them. Taking a piece of the cheese, also from the store, diced some into very small pieces. Then, going out to the smoke house, Olga retrieved one of the smoked hams hanging there and carried it in the house.

Betsy and Kathryn, busy in the bedroom, heard Olga banging around in the kitchen and were soon there with her, helping her prepare a meal for them all.

Being unaware that the smokehouse was stocked, Kathryn was shocked to see the ham laying on the counter. There was a lot of chat and laughter coming from the kitchen area. Vernon Knott and Ponder had been outdoors, inspecting the barn and admiring the stock they could readily see. They had seen Olga carrying the ham from the smokehouse to inside the house and Ponder was surprised, as he had no idea the smokehouse had anything in it. He didn't know much about a smokehouse except that he had seen many of them. Walking back towards the house, Knott commented that it was a really nice place. He mentioned to Ponder that he had hoped someday to have a place such as this one. Ponder considered that. The Knott's were nice folks and had become quick friends with him and Kathryn.

"Knott," Ponder said, "If you and Betsy would like to live out here, there is no reason you couldn't build a place right over there," pointing at an area fairly close to the entrance to the property. "I don't know if the traffic would bear it, but you could even move your store there as well."

"You can't be serious," said Knott with a shocked look about him. "There is no way that I can afford to buy that land from you."

"Not asking you to Knott. Y'all have been like family to us the past few days and I am certain that Kathryn would enjoy you being on this place with us."

"Ponder," said Knott, "I am overwhelmed with your graciousness. I'm going to have to think about your offer and see what Betsy thinks about it."

"Besides Knott," said Ponder, "It's going to be hard for one man to make this place work."

Soon, Kathryn found Knott and Ponder and reported that lunch was ready. They followed her back into the house where the kitchen table was set with Olga's plates and such. A plate of sliced, warmed, smoked ham was on the table as well as a bowl of boiled and mashed potatoes that had bits of cheese mixed into them. No apple cider today, but glasses with water taken from the pipe that brought it from the spring behind the house.

Although the only person at the table that could truly understand her was Betsy, Olga was excitedly carrying on, pointing every which way direction talking about "their" new home. Betsy was relaying the basics of what Olga was saying. In time, they would understand one another's speech better. Before everyone ate, Knott raised his glass of water in a toast, joined by the rest, wishing the best for the Ponders, which now included Olga Ulrich.

The meal was wonderful and seemingly enjoyed by them all. It was a new world for Ponder and Kathryn and surely for Olga. And perhaps even for Vernon and Betsy because even they felt as if they were with family.

Lunch was over and the women were busy clearing the table and again were talking and laughing as they went about. Ponder was captivated with it all. This was an experience he had never partaken of, and he liked it. *This is what it should be like*, he thought.

After a while, the women seemed to be done in the kitchen, came out, and were walking through the house going through all the rooms again, upstairs and down with things like "you could" or "might be" being said often. Olga was in on it too as she was chattering just like Kathryn and Betsy were. Three happy women!

Kathryn was no longer that whipped, lost young lady at the Guadalupe. She seemed to be where it was that she should be. Ponder felt the same way. He thought that both of them were in the right place.

But in a while, Knott, looking at his time piece, grudgingly told Betsy that they were going to need to head back to Llano soon.

"I know," said Betsy. You could tell from her expression that leaving was somewhat of a disappointment.

Standing up, Ponder walked to Knott, shook his hand and thanked him for helping them move. He also went to Betsy and gave her a good hug, looking her in the face and telling her that he did not know what they would have done without her. With a bit of sadness, the Knotts boarded their wagon and, waving hands as in goodbye, rode away, headed back to Llano.

Chapter 27

⋯⟵⟶⋯

Home at Last

It had been a busy but fun day. Ponder, when seeing Kathryn come past him, thought that she in no way resembled the desperate, defeated woman he first saw on the bank of the Guadalupe a few days prior. And then realizing that everything and more that he had ever dreamed of having was all bundled up, right here, right now before his eyes.

Next time Kathryn came through, she came straight to him and held him tightly with her head next to his.

She whispered to him that she was the luckiest woman alive to have found him, "Every dream that I have ever had has come true because of you Ponder."

"And mine as well Kathryn," he said softly. "Let's make the best of it."

That evening, Olga warmed up some of the ham from lunch and the leftover potatoes as well. Prior to that, she had made a pie crust and filled it with peaches from a can, put a lattice top on it, and baked it in what was her new oven. When the three of them sat down to have supper, Ponder could still see the happiness on Olga's face. He mentioned to her that if she kept feeding him like this, he was going to be a fat man. With this, Olga laughed. Ponder did not know whether she understood what he said or not. On the other hand, it sure beat canned beans and fire dried meat. He liked the presence of Olga. Olga was going to be good for Kathryn, and him as well.

After the dishes were cleaned up from supper, Olga somewhat indicated that she was tired and retreated up the stairs to what was her new bedroom.

Ponder asked Kathryn if she would like to get some rest.

111

"Maybe some," Kathryn answered.

After latching the doors and shutters, Ponder carried the lighted candle from the kitchen table to their bedroom. Entering the bedroom, he could see Kathryn washing herself with a cloth that had been hanging on a rack just above the wash bowl.

"Just a minute," Kathryn said. "When I get through, I will wash you."

Something smelled really nice in the room and Ponder commented on it.

"It's the soap Ponder. I hope that you don't mind, but I bought some of it at Knott's this morning. It's called 'eau de fleur'. I think that it is French soap."

"Kathryn, if you smell like that when we go to bed, I am liable to sniff you all night."

"Well hell then, let me use some more of it," Kathryn said, laughing. She finished washing and motioned Ponder to the chest with the wash basin on it. He removed his boots and clothing and tossed them aside. He then stood there for a very long time, enjoying the bath he was being given by this beautiful naked woman to whom he was married.

"Kathryn," he said softly, "Will it always be like this?"

"Does this feel good my dearest Ponder?" she asked.

"Yes," answered Ponder.

Kathryn replied softly, "Then you are really going to like what I have in store for you on that bed tonight. And Ponder, you deserve every bit of it." She finished washing Ponder and then gently toweled him dry. After hanging the towel, she went and laid on the bed and said sweetly, "Come here and I will show you Ponder."

When they finally embraced and were going to sleep, Ponder wondered somehow if Kathryn had ever really had anyone love her, sexually or otherwise. He had never seen a person so hungry for love, or even just friendship. He went to sleep wondering what her life before had been like. He might inquire sometime later about that, but now was not the time. He had no wish to possibly squash the happiness she now seemed to have. He really didn't care about the "before" of Kathryn. He was too delighted with the "now" of her.

Chapter 28

⊷═◉═⊷

The Morning Came — and Many More

"Do you smell that that?" were the words said by Kathryn the first morning as he was waking. "It must be Olga. Good Lord what is she cooking?" Slipping her dress on, Kathryn was off like a rabbit towards the kitchen.

Ponder noticed the smell of bacon frying and something else also. In a moment, Kathryn came running back through the door saying that Olga was frying bacon, making pancakes and syrup, and has milked the goat, and she was gone again toward the kitchen where he could hear she and Olga talking and laughing. It was like Kathryn was a small child in the kitchen with her mother on Christmas day.

The breakfast was one for kings. Olga had milked the goats and had set some in the spring in a pitcher to cool. The pancakes were light as air. She had cooked some sugar down in water on the stove and made syrup and had seasoned it with something she found near the spring. The bacon was crisp and well cooked. He had never been much of a milk drinker, but he enjoyed the goat's milk. Ponder was convinced that there was a conspiracy to feed him to death. Goodness, had he someone to pick his teeth, he would have it all.

About noon, Ponder heard some horse hooves hitting ground and then heard a voice say, "Hey you inside, come out here".

As Ponder walked toward the front door, he placed the Navy in his waist, left side, with the butt to the left. Stepping out the door and onto the porch, he looked at each of the three men there on horseback. They reminded him

113

of some of the men he had seen in Sedalia. The ones that were trying to take, for nothing, what another man had worked for.

"What ever can I do for you?" said Ponder.

"We're taking a head of your cattle. That's what we are doing here farmer," the man on the right said.

"Is that a fact?" replied Ponder. "I plumb forgot that I was giving one away. I've been told there were three types of scum around here right now. One was outlaws. The second were vigilantes that call themselves "The Mob" and the third were some carpet baggers from up north. Which of those would you three assholes be?"

From the house, a female voice said, "Ponder? Do you want me to bark the one on the right or just shoot him outright."

Before Ponder could even reply there was the 'pow' sound of a Henry .44 and the rider on the right's hat flew from his head with a piece of the man's head inside it. Palming the Navy, as the other two riders were on the backs of horses bucking because of the gunfire, Ponder took the other two. Turning, he saw Kathryn standing in the window by the dining table, with the Henry in her hands.

"Good shot Kat," said Ponder. "I couldn't have done better myself."

Olga then walked out onto the porch and made a sign as if punching her left palm with her right fist. *Well*, Ponder thought, *looks like I have plenty of backup. Good thing I had a good breakfast, because I have to bury these three pieces of trash.*

Olga walked out to where the three men lay and pulled their boots off. She also went through their clothing and found two pocket watches and several dollars in coin. Meanwhile, Ponder took the reins of the three men's horses and led them to the corral where he stripped the saddles and all from them and carried the saddles in the barn, placing them on a rail inside, designed for such.

Olga had gathered everything of value from the dead bodies and had their firearms, carrying them into the house. Ponder hitched one of the dead men's horses to the wagon, retrieved a shovel from the barn, and led the horse pulling the wagon to the front of the house.

He picked each outlaw or, whatever they were, up and placed them in the wagon bed. Boarding the wagon, he carried the dead guys out of the front of the property and stopped in the road that they had come there on. He got out, rolled his sleeves, and started digging. Thinking that these three were good friends, he was just going to dig one hole, place all three in it, and let them rest together.

The ground was very rocky, so it was tough digging. Ponder pulled the three bodies from the wagon and to the grave he dug, noticing that the one that Kathryn shot had seemed to have a shocked look on his face. It wasn't long and he had the wagon back to the barn, horse unhitched and back in the corral. Stopping at the water trough, he rinsed his hands and shook the water from them as he headed to the house. Once entering, he was met by Olga with a fresh cup of coffee.

"Thanks for the coffee Olga and the breakfast too."

Olga smiled and said perfectly, "You are welcome."

Chapter 29

⊷══⊶

What Do We Have

After having the coffee and visiting with Kathryn, he went out to saddle Lilly. He spent some time brushing her with his hand and talking to her before putting a blanket and saddle on her. She was a good horse and had carried him far.

"Lilly," he said, "Let's go get a good look at this place," and they did.

Ponder just sort of wandered with Lilly, going from one property marker to the next. Although the place was mostly unfit for much cultivation, he really liked the lay of it. The house was backed by a fair size mountain and to the front of the house was a nice meadow of sorts, plus the four or so acres that had been cultivated. Past that, a gentle rise of rock formations started about at the edge of their property line. There were all sorts of trees, brush, and grasses. There were some really large oak trees on the place and he could tell that several had been cut down, probably for the wood to build the house and other buildings, however they were mostly rock.

He saw a lot of evidence that there were deer, rabbits, and turkey on the place. *No excuse for starving on this place*, he thought. The stock this morning were grazing near the extreme front of the valley that was visible from the front of the house. Riding around the cattle, they seemed to be healthy and were fat from having so much forage in late summer.

Looking back towards the house, he could see Kathryn with a bucket of grain taken from the barn, walking around in her yard, feeding the chickens. A bit of smoke rising from the chimney where the kitchen was told him that

Olga was preparing something for later in the day. In front of the house, he stepped from Lilly and walked her to the barn door where he unsaddled her.

With the saddle, blanket, and bridle dropped to the ground, standing in front of Lilly, he said, "Girl, we are home," and left her free to go where she pleased.

He carried the things taken from Lilly to the barn, placing them where they were supposed to be stored. As he was walking from the barn, he saw Kathryn running towards him.

She landed on him with her legs around his waist and arms around his neck and said, "We're home Ponder. We're home."